A LAMP FOR NIGHTFALL

by

Erskine Caldwell

Duell, Sloan and Pearce · *New York*

Little, Brown and Company · *Boston*

DUELL, SLOAN AND PEARCE — LITTLE, BROWN
BOOKS ARE PUBLISHED BY
LITTLE, BROWN AND COMPANY
IN ASSOCIATION WITH
DUELL, SLOAN & PEARCE, INC.

Published simultaneously
in Canada by McClelland and Stewart Limited

PRINTED IN THE UNITED STATES OF AMERICA

A LAMP FOR NIGHTFALL

CHAPTER I

~~~~~~

For more than an hour before getting out of his automobile to go into Robinson's store, Thede Emerson sat gazing down the sun-shadowed street of the village. The porchless, white-clapboarded, salt-box houses along both sides of the winding street gleamed in the warm sun like crusted drifts of late-winter snow.

Thede glanced thoughtfully at the coach-and-four weather vane on a rooftop across the street, his mind uneasy about the next day's weather, but there was not enough force in the breeze to enable him to gauge its direction. He had admitted to himself many times that he liked such pleasant days in early June when Clearwater was not overrun with summer-people; but now he was too angry to be pleased with anything anywhere. He hated every person and every object he could lay his eyes on.

What displeased him the most was the sight of Hormidas Doucette, the postmaster, sitting at ease in a comfortable chair on the post-office porch, and, like a presumptuous foreigner, smiling neighborly at him. Thede had been watching the postmaster from the corners of his eyes ever since he had driven into the village street and stopped near Robinson's store, but not once had he allowed himself to turn his face in Doucette's direction. He did not care to have Hormidas Doucette, or anyone with such a foreign-sounding name, speaking to him.

Thede knew that Doucette had as much right to smile at him as he had to scowl at Doucette, but what made him more angry than ever was the friendly way in which the postmaster tried to be pleasant. He had never yet spoken directly to Doucette and, should he see the Frenchman every day for the next twenty years, Thede was determined that he would never open his mouth in Hormidas Doucette's presence.

He glanced behind the automobile to see if there was anyone to whom he could say what he thought of Doucette. A man was crossing the street from the barbershop, Without waiting to look closely enough to see that it was Napoleon St. Denis, Thede began talking. It was the first opportunity to express himself fully that he had had in a long time.

St. Denis was walking slowly across the street toward Thede and the automobile.

"This State of Maine has come to a devil of a pass when we pay our taxes to support Canucks and other foreigners in federal offices. That Doucette sits there reared back in a comfortable chair looking just like he owned the post office, instead of conducting himself like a public jobholder ought to."

Thede had just got started when he recognized Napoleon St. Denis. He was angry with himself for speaking to St. Denis, but he had so much he wanted to say, and he wished so badly to say it, that he paused for only a moment. Napoleon St. Denis continued slowly along the street by the side of the car.

"The next thing we know, the squareheads and Canucks and hunkies will be up and deporting the true townsmen from the country. They'd like to do it now, but they've got sense enough to know it's not time yet. The time will come a little later on, when they're outvoting us at the polls five to one. Between the sporting summer-people and the Canucks, I wouldn't give a cellarful of rotten apples for the whole state if it was offered to me — and the reason they don't offer it is because they know there'd be no takers. The only fitting thing for us true townsmen to do in this day and time is be dead. The foreigners wouldn't stop to take the time and trouble to dig us up out of our graves and ship us out of the country. They'd be too busy sporting around in their big autos and collecting pay in the federal offices to bother."

"*Baste! Ce faneur abruti! On doit envoyer promener ce canaille-là! Mais, après tout, il ne peut pas faire du mal à personne.*"

Thede glanced out into the street at St. Denis. It made him more angry than ever to realize that he had been talking all that time to a Frenchman, who had answered him in words he could not understand, but he was glad to have had the chance to say what he wished. St. Denis went up the street toward his house without looking back again.

"We'll all be jabbering Canuck talk ten-eleven years from now," Thede said, raising his voice with his final words to St. Denis.

[5]

Turning, he squinted from the corners of his eyes at Hormidas Doucette across the street and then he spat upon the ground. He thought much less than that of a French-speaking Canadian from Quebec.

"Never thought I'd live to see the time when one of those Frenchmen would be handling my mail in Clearwater Town, and grinning about being the government postmaster all the while he's doing it."

For the first time since he had stopped his car in the village street he noticed the herd of Hereford cattle grazing on the pasture slope that rose from the end of the street a quarter of a mile away. As he watched the steers, Thede's heart beat faster, and a slow smile spread across his face. His own cattle out at the farm had once looked as fine as that herd, even finer. But he had the money put away safely, the money that the cattle had brought, and he would not exchange what he had now for any number of cows and steers, even if he could get the finest stock in the whole country. He would take his choice any day between two hundred thousand dollars and a herd of cattle.

Still, the grazing cattle on the hillside brought a grim twist to the corners of his mouth as he remembered the stock and dairy farm at Autumn Hill. He would never be able to forget those forty years, because the money he now had would always remind him of the animals he had exchanged for it.

Slowly the realization came to him that the cattle on the hill belonged to Napoleon Fortiner, the Frenchman who had bought the abandoned Thaxter farm and who called himself a Franco-American. And the smile on

Thede's face became set in lines as grim as graven stone. He hurriedly got out of his car before he could see the Hereford herd again.

"God stopped having pity on us when He let all those foreigners into the country," he said, glancing at Hormidas Doucette once more from the corners of his eyes. "They've already taken the best farms and the best political jobs away from us, and we'll all be working and sweating for them inside another ten years, if there're any of the true townsmen left by that time."

After having said what he had been wanting to say aloud on the public street for the past two weeks, Thede spat again on the ground and went into Robinson's store. Robinson's store was the last refuge of the townsmen; it was the only place left in the village where he would not have to breathe the common air with a Frenchman or a Scandinavian.

When Thede walked through the door, there were ten or twelve men sitting in chairs and on the counters. Two or three were talking, some were listening to what was being discussed, and several others were waiting for an opportunity to express themselves. Ben Robinson, the owner of the store, was sitting in his buggy-back chair, chewing and listening.

Whatever the subject was that had been under discussion, the men stopped talking abruptly when Thede came in and walked down through the store nodding to Ben and to one or two others. Ben threw up a hand in greeting, letting it fall back to his knees without effort.

For several moments the store was quiet. The men seemed to be waiting for Thede to speak first. He had

[7]

not yet publicly expressed his views on the subject of the approaching marriage of his daughter, Jean, and everyone was eager to hear Thede state his position. And coming from Thede Emerson, it was generally believed that it would undoubtedly be a statement worth hearing. Still no one spoke, though several of the men began to nod at one another and to clear their throats. Thede looked around the store, noting the familiar faces in the roughly formed circle. He had to be sure that he was among his own people before he would allow himself to say a word.

"They tell me that you're planning on conducting a wedding out at Autumn Hill, come fall," Ben Robinson said, looking at every man in the store except Thede.

Everyone else looked at Thede, but there was no indication on his face that he had heard what Ben said.

"I said," Ben repeated, his voice resounding up and down the store, "that they tell me you're proposing to hold a wedding out at Autumn Hill, come fall."

By the time he had finished, Ben's raised voice was loud enough to have been heard outside in the street.

"Heard you," Thede said, speaking for the first time since he had entered the building. "Not hard of hearing."

"Knew you heard me the first time," Ben said, winking at some of the others, "but I figured that maybe you didn't know what I was talking about."

"Do you?" Thede said.

"If I don't know, there's any number here in the store who can tell you."

"Maybe there is any number here in the store who

[8]

think they could tell me," Thede replied, "but it wouldn't be anything new to me."

Now that Ben and Thede had greeted each other with their customary banter, the other men settled down to hear about the wedding that had been set for October, almost five months away.

"Everybody's invited to come out to the wedding," Thede said, extending his arms expansively. "Yes, everybody. Don't care who you are. Don't care if you're half Finn and half petered-out American, or part squarehead and part Canuck — with a little Hereford thrown in. There's going to be a big wedding at Autumn Hall in the fall, and I should like everybody in the town of Clearwater to come to see my girl get married. Only got one daughter to marry off, and I'm going to have it done in the finest style. It's going to be the biggest wedding party any of you have ever seen or heard about. Guess maybe it will be the finest that ever took place in the town."

Several men coughed; one scraped his feet on the floor.

"Who's she going to marry, Thede?" a man, who carefully hid his face, asked in a thin voice.

Thede stood up, his face crimson and his hands trembling. He glared at Ben, at Lincoln Burton, at Arthur White, and at several others nearest to him.

"You know blamed well who she's going to marry, whoever you are that's saying that and scared to show yourself, and so does everybody else in town!" he shouted. "What if she is going to marry a Frenchman! By God, the whole state will be Canuck, with a little Russian and rat thrown in, in another ten-eleven years! Sure, I'm letting her marry a Canuck. That breed and the square-heads are paying all the taxes now just about, being as how nearly everybody else has stopped working and gone to living on the town. If I were to make her marry a petered-out American, by God, they'd both starve to death before the winter was half over."

Now that Thede had begun to express himself fully and unmistakably on the subject, the men around the store sat up and waited for what they knew was certain to follow. When Thede Emerson had once made up his mind to take a definite stand, he always gave everybody within hearing of his voice the opportunity of knowing exactly what he thought about the matter. Moreover, the fact that his daughter was marrying a Frenchman, in spite of his well-known prejudice against French Canadians, called for every word of explanation he could make.

"Did I hear you inviting Swedes and Finns to the wedding, Thede?" Ben asked, raising his voice for the benefit of everybody else in the store. "It don't sound like Thede Emerson to be asking Erik Hedenstjerna and Alarak Henata and such foreigners to his house, not to mention the French. I'm surprised to hear that you've taken a liking to the foreigners, Thede. Something's come over you. You're a changed man, Thede."

"I'm giving the invitation to everybody who has ears to hear me," Thede answered in a firm voice. "Won't be holding grudges against the French and Scandinavians, not even against the Portuguese, at a time like this. Those Canucks have been sons-of-bitches heretofore and likely will be forever after, but when my girl is getting married,

I want that everybody in the whole town should come and see her and drink my hard cider. Everybody is invited. Yes, the foreigners, too, just as much as the people who've got names I can pronounce. I'm not slighting any breed of man who can stand up and walk on two hind legs."

"Now, wait a minute," Arthur said. "There're some things about all this I don't understand. Let me get it straight in my mind. You said you're inviting everybody in the town to go over to your place and drink your cider with you while your daughter is marrying Frank Gervais, didn't you?"

"That's what I said and I meant it," Thede said. "And I'm not the kind who backs down, either. Don't have to say it more than once, do I?"

"Never mind about that, Thede," Arthur said. "What I'm getting after is this: If we're all going to be at Autumn Hill drinking your cider — and it had better be good, and hard, too — who's going to be holding the gun on Frank Gervais?"

"By God," Thede shouted angrily, getting red in the face again, "nobody's going to be doing it! My girl and the boy are getting married because they have a mind to. I'll be blamed if it's not getting so nowadays that a man can't marry off his daughter without having a lot of store-counter potato farmers saying there's something peculiar about it. It had better be stopped now once and for all. The libel laws of this state are still on the books, and there's a lawyer-friend of mine in Lewiston who knows how to use them. I'd sue a man for saying less than that, if it was willfully repeated a second time after due warning, and I don't mean for a niggardly hundred dollars, either. Wouldn't be satisfied for getting less than fifty thousand."

"Now, Thede," Lincoln said, "don't go and get all het up like that. You know good and well that the boys just had to have their little joke. They didn't mean anything personal, either about you or the girl. You're not the first one with a daughter to marry off who's had to sit still and take it. You know we didn't mean it any other way at all."

"Well, by God, I'm getting blamed tired of hearing people, mostly behind my back, say it's about time for Jean to get married, if she can. Well, for and by God, she can and she is going to!"

"Always heard it said," a man in the rear of the circle said quietly, "that it was the man who upset the girl that had to marry her. Maybe that lets Frank Gervais out, and maybe it don't."

Thede did not hear what had been said, and he waited to hear what Lincoln was going to say in reply.

"Jean's a fine girl," Lincoln said after a while. "We all know that, Thede. Now, let's none of us harbor any ill feelings about this thing. It all came up to make a joke."

Thede was nodding slowly. Presently he looked up, his lips parted with a broad smile.

"Not holding it against anybody for talking about my daughter now," he said. "She might have a young one that will be the blamest nine-months-wonder a man ever saw or heard of, but all the same she's getting married come fall."

"There's no sense in taking it that way," Lincoln said. "You ought to know better than that, Thede."

"It's nobody's business but my own how I wish to take it. But, as I said, I'm not holding it against any man, so far. Still would like to have everybody come out to Autumn Hill in October and be at the wedding and drink my good cider."

Ben Robinson returned from selling a customer a box of matches and sat down in his buggy-backed chair near Thede.

"There's one thing about all this marrying I can't understand as a man my age should. It's about the boy Jean's going to marry, Thede."

"What about him?"

"Well, Frank Gervais is French — Franco-Americans, they call themselves. He was born right here in the town, as we all know, but his parents came here from Canada — from Quebec Province, I've been told. They were foreigners, and still are, if you wish to look at it that way. Now, how comes it that you are letting your daughter marry a Frenchman, knowing as everybody does what you've been saying about such people since they began moving in here like they have for the past ten-twenty years? Have you changed your mind and opinions about the Canucks, Thede?"

"You know I haven't changed my mind a fraction of an inch, Ben Robinson. Got more use for the rats and the woodchucks than I have for Onesime Dube or Napoleon St. Denis, or any of the others you could name, including the squareheads. But this is different, by the looks of what I've figured out. If I stopped the marriage, they would either run off somewhere together, or else wouldn't marry at all. You see how that is, don't you?"

"Mostly," Ben said.

"Don't care to have either of those two things to happen," Thede stated. "If they ran off somewhere and got married, it would be no different from my letting them marry at Autumn Hill. They would be married, and would start living together. Then, on the other hand, if they didn't marry, I figure that maybe Jean wouldn't marry anybody else.—"

"Or couldn't," somebody said.

"Yes, couldn't. Maybe she would like to and couldn't. Well, in that case she would stay at home and I'd be put to a continued expense for her board and clothes. So, being set against having to take that risk, I told her she could go ahead and marry the boy in the fall. Don't make any allowances for the fact that he's a Frenchman, beyond what I've already told you. Told you that when I came in her a little while ago. A Frenchman will feed and clothe her. An American would marry her and they'd both starve to death before spring, if they didn't freeze to death first. Couldn't afford to support two of them, no more than I can afford to support her any longer than October. So, as it is, I'm getting her off my hands, knowing there will be no demands for food and money in the future. I'm satisfied with the bargain, she's satisfied and more, and I guess everybody else in town ought to be satisfied too, being as how it's none of their business to begin with. Jean has said that she wouldn't marry anybody else, if she couldn't marry him. So now everybody is satisfied. She's getting what she wishes, and I'll have one less mouth to feed after October."

"Guess you'll end up getting chummy with your new

in-laws," Ben said. "Didn't expect to live to see the day come when you'd get chummy with the French."

"I will not! I've got just as much use for a Frenchman as I have for a cellarful of rotten potatoes."

"Appreciate your invitation to the wedding, anyway," Ben said. "I thank you from the bottom of my heart for asking me to come to Autumn Hill and drink your good cider and watch your daughter get married, and I guess everybody else feels the same as I do about it. We'll be there. But there's one thing I should like to say to you in your face before I go out to your house at Autumn Hill in the fall."

"What's that?" he asked.

"I'm good and glad, Thede Emerson, that you're getting a dose of your own brand of medicine for once. You've been talking about the females in this town for well on to fifty years, as I recall, telling everybody, and summer-people into the bargain, as how the girls and women sometimes have to hustle around between sunset and sunrise and cajole a man to marry them in a pretty quick hurry, and that more often than not the only man they could get was a foreigner. Now all that talk and gossip is coming back at you. You're getting what you've been giving all these years."

Ben paused, giving Thede an opportunity to say something, but Thede remained silent.

"Personally," Ben said after a while, "I'm giving you the benefit of the doubt this time, Thede. I've had my say now, and I can be quiet about it from now on. You ought to be thankful about that, because you know how I can keep a matter alive when I have a mind to. But I can't help it if everybody else in the town talks about your girl and says she had to do it to take precaution, and that she couldn't find anybody but a Frenchman who would marry her. That's what you're deserving of, Thede. By rights, it's coming to you."

"I'm getting old," Thede said. "Can't argue with a storeful of men like I used to. So we'll just drop everything where it is now and not make a lot of enemies among ourselves by discussing it. All I want to say now is that I'm looking for everybody out to Autumn Hill for the wedding. Don't wish anybody in Clearwater Town, friend or enemy, to miss attending a big celebration like that at my house, especially when I've got nine barrels of last-crop cider waiting to be passed around. By October all the summer-people will have come and gone again, thank God, and won't none of the townsmen be taking the risk of getting run over on the road to Autumn Hill by a flock of big autos that we can't assess and collect taxes on."

CHAPTER II

THEDE TURNED SLOWLY AND, WALKING STIFFLY TO THE front of the store, stood looking out the window at Hormidas Doucette, who apparently had not moved from his comfortable chair during the past hour. Thede was again concerned and upset by what he saw; he would never be able to change his belief that any man who held a job, and especially a public job provided for by town or government taxes, should always make a stir of doing something, even if he only turned over papers or swept the floor or stood on his feet during the hours of his employment.

He disliked Doucette then as much as ever, but while he stood there gazing across the street at the post office, he could not keep from feeling that somehow Doucette was, after all, as capable of performing the duties of postmaster as anyone else would be. The only trouble with Hormidas Doucette was that he was a Frenchman, and Thede could never forgive that in a man.

Not turning around to see who was standing behind him, Thede said again, more to himself than to Arthur White, "Well, my son-in-law will be a Canuck, but, by God, I won't have to feed and house them. If Jean had been marrying a Robinson or a Frost, or some other petered-out American, they'd starve to death before middlemost winter. There's fourteen-fifteen people with such names living completely on the town now, or else drawing eleven-twelve dollars a month from the town poor fund to keep themselves alive. But there's never been a Nordenskjold or a Hammarstand to come begging for the town's help. Jean is pretty well off, I guess. If she had been marrying a Hopkins, God help her, because nobody else would."

"When you were calling off those names just a minute ago, Thede," Arthur said, "you overlooked naming the Emerson family."

"Guess you're right, at that," Thede said. "Outside of me and my own household, the Emersons are no better than the rest of them. But I'm not giving those with the Emerson name anything of mine to keep them off the town. I got myself to look after. One of those Emersons over in Clearwater Mills talked me into loaning him two hundred dollars once, and I wasted the whole of three years running over there and back, three-four times a month, keeping the interest paid up. But I'd never do a fool thing like that again, even for my own brother."

"Now that your girl is marrying and leaving home, what about the boy?" Arthur said. "I've heard that Howard would like to go off to college and study engineering. Guess you've made up your mind for what you'd like him to do, haven't you?"

"He's working on the town roads this summer," Thede said. "He worried me almost out of my mind to let him do it, and I let him take a job. But when you talk about him going to college, not by my leave he won't. And I've already told him so. Not that he'll believe me and stop thinking about it all the time. He believes he's saving his money now to spend at a school somewhere. He'll find out this fall, though, if he doesn't learn some sense before that time. He'll be doing the chores at Autumn Hill from then on. There's no sense in my paying a hired man twenty dollars a week and board to do chores. When Howard came to me this spring and said he would like to go work on the roads this summer, I told him to go ahead and do it, and to save his money. He makes five dollars a day, which is right good wages for a boy nineteen years old, Arthur."

"He's big and husky enough to earn them. There's six-seven men working on the town roads right now who can't do any more labor than Howard."

"That's all right then, so far. But when he started talking about going off to college and spending five-six hundred dollars to get in, not to mention the board and housing, that was where I told him never mind talking about it any more. He can learn all he needs to know about building roads and bridges working right here in the town, getting five dollars a day besides; but when he said that about going off somewhere to college and paying five-six hundred dollars just to get inside, I haven't got the time to waste listening."

"Can see how you feel about it, Thede, but it's going to be hard on the boy. Heard him talking about it one day not so long ago, and he said that if you wouldn't let him have the money, he was going to work on the roads till he got enough saved up for a year's study. Now, that's pretty hard, Thede. You take a boy nineteen years old and bend him to man's labor five-six years, and it sort of takes all the spirit out of him. He's not fit for anything else, except doing the same thing over again for the rest of his life. Howard is your boy and I'm not trying to tell you what to do, but it looks to me like a man as wealthy as you are ought to give him his education. You banked around two hundred thousand dollars from selling your dairy and beef cattle, didn't you?"

"And keeping it where I put it," Thede said. "I'm not taking out five-six hundred dollars to throw away. And besides, I can't let him go off to college; he's got to stay at home and do the chores. I can get around all right in summer, but when snow covers the ground, I can't afford to get out and do such work. I've got to stay on the inside and keep off the ice. Howard ought to stay here and work the farm, and that's what he is going to do."

"That may be partly so, Thede, but just look at what has happened to the other young people of the town. They didn't wish to stay, and they didn't. They went up to Boston, and some of them over to New York, and I hear they're all doing well. They didn't have a college education. They only went through the village high school like Howard. Well, if they could go off and do all of that, don't you guess your boy could do a lot more when he goes off if he had that engineering education to help him along? There's no sense in saying what he and the rest of the young people ought to do. We should find out what it is they want and then help them get it. That'll save Clearwater from the foreigners quicker than anything else."

"No use talking about it, Arthur," Thede said. "I'm holding on to what I've got. The boy has got to scramble for his own, if he'd like to have some."

"He's not after making a lot of money, Thede. He hopes to build bridges. There's a lot of difference in the two. Don't guess you can see it that way, but Howard isn't after what you've got. He would like to build things."

"When you hear tell that I've started taking good money out of the bank to send Howard off to learn how to build bridges, you can come and take me off to the State Hospital, because I'll be a good and tried candidate for it."

That seemed to settle the matter as far as Thede himself was concerned, and Arthur did not feel like arguing with him any longer. No one had ever induced Thede Emerson to change his mind once he had made it up, and Arthur knew that as well as anyone else in town.

They walked back to the rear of the store where Ben Robinson and the other men were talking. Thede sat down and filled his pipe.

"Heard somebody say he saw Jake Thaxter walking up the back road on the other side of the lake early this morning," Ben said, looking at Arthur. "Maybe you know what Jake was doing up there, Arthur."

Arthur glanced at the faces to see who was present and who was not present in the store. He had become careful in whose presence he spoke ever since a man from the north part of town had threatened to take him before a law court for talking about his wife.

"Today wasn't the first time Jake Thaxter has been over on that back road," Arthur said. "Guess he goes over there pretty often nowadays. Only two-three days ago I was driving my horse and cart along the lane and I saw Jake's head sticking up over a stone wall near the Smith place. Guess Jake's taken to living around Oscar Smith's rented house of late — on the outside."

"Jake won't learn anything he don't already know by hiding behind stone walls," Ben said. "Jake ought to have the wisdom to know that. The thing for him to do is to creep closer to those shored-up buildings if he has a mind to spy some. Then he'd be mistaken for the forest closing in, and he could stand there three-four days at a time while Oscar was thinking Jake was a new-growth fir tree that had sprung up overnight."

Nearly every person in the town knew by that time that Jake Thaxter's youngish wife had left him to live with Oscar Smith. Jake did not mind losing her as much as he regretted the fact that Oscar did not own anything of value that could be attached if he were to bring suit against him. Oscar lived on a rented farm and he had neither an automobile nor a horse, and neither did he have money in the bank. He had boarded at Jake Thaxter's for about six months, until Jake decided that he had stood as much from Oscar as he cared to stand, and had told Oscar to get out of his house and to stay out thereafter.

Oscar had acquired a habit, during the half-year he lived in Jake's house, of coming home late in the evening and ordering Jake to get up out of bed and spend the rest of the night on the couch in the kitchen. Jake had put up with it until cold weather came and, as he had been accustomed to sleeping with his wife for nearly ten years, he at last took the stand that he was not going to get up out of a warm bed on a wintry night to let Oscar Smith get into it. Jake's wife, Edna, protested for a while, because she had encouraged Oscar by saying she had no objection to his making Jake sleep on the kitchen couch, but Jake himself remained firm and unyielding in attitude. He flatly refused to get out of bed one night to let Oscar get into it, and a week later Oscar rented a house and twenty acres of tillage. A few days later, Edna packed her belongings and went to live with him. She and Oscar had been living together there on the rented farm since April of that year.

"Well, I'll tell you," Arthur said. "Jake is just waiting now for the time when Oscar makes a little something, and maybe buys an automobile or something, and then he's going to bring suit and try to get a judgment against Oscar for enticing Edna away from him. He'll sue for divorce, too, so he'll be certain of getting a judgment. He's got a deep-rooted grudge against Edna and Oscar now, because she said he was petered-out and that she needed Oscar to take his place. On top of that, he's still good and mad because Oscar used to make him get out of a warm bed in middlemost winter. Can't say I blame him any, either. If me and my wife had a boarder who took to demanding the privilege, I'd do the same thing Jake's trying to do, only I'd be a little more active about it. I'd only be satisfied when I had sued, and sued for all he was worth and ever would be."

Thede crossed and recrossed his legs restlessly. He knew all about Jake's trouble with Edna and Oscar, as did everyone else in the town who had taken the trouble to listen to the gossip, and the matter annoyed him. There was not a man in Clearwater who did not know that Thede and Rosa, Thede's wife, had had trouble of the same nature for the past several years. Lately Rosa had been meeting Leland Stokes, who was a part-time butcher by trade, and Thede did not know how to put a stop to it, much less how to silence the town gossip. Rosa was twenty years younger than Thede, and he had never succeeded in dominating her. She had always done as she wished, and most of the things she did displeased Thede. However, Rosa was a good housekeeper, and he did not like to think of having to pay another woman thirty or forty dollars a month and board to keep house for him when Rosa's services cost him next to nothing.

"What would you do in Jake Thaxter's shoes, Thede?" Ben asked pointedly.

Thede shook his head, refusing to answer.

"But suppose your wife started letting a hired man run you out of a warm bed on cold nights so he could get into it. You know you'd do something drastic, now wouldn't you, Thede?"

Thede scowled at Ben and the others, knowing that he could no longer refuse to make some reply.

"I'd get me another woman," Thede said at last.

"But suppose you liked the one you had — what would you do then?"

"Wouldn't be after suing him."

"Then what would you do, Thede?" Arthur asked insistingly.

"Take after him and run him off to Canada," Thede said. "And then maybe after I'd got him up there, all winded and broken-shoed, I'd shoot him. Would shoot him just as I would a pesky woodchuck sitting in my vegetable garden."

Presently one of the men on the other side of the store walked across the floor and back.

"They tell me that Leland Stokes is up to something with a married woman these days," he said. "Don't know what woman he's seeing, but I'd say he's keeping long hours, because I've seen him real early in the morning, just at sunrise, hustling back to the village from somewhere. I'd make a guess that he's seeing a woman in the west part of the town. That's the direction he's coming from every time I see him. Wouldn't say it's anything new for Leland Stokes to be doing, though. He's been providing part-time company for some woman for most of the past twenty years."

This was not news to anyone, not even to Thede. For several months Rosa had been leaving the house, sometimes at night and sometimes during the day, to meet Leland, and Thede had been aware of it all the time. He had hoped, though, that the affair would either come to an end quickly, or else would cease to be a topic of conversation all over the town. He knew of no way to make Rosa stop seeing Leland. She had often said she would move out of the house before she would obey him.

"It looks like something of the kind is going on all the time," Arthur said. "And nine times out of ten it's likely to be native Americans, and not the foreigners, who're doing it. Now, you take Stephen Frost, who used to live down toward East Webster, near the town line. When Stephen Frost died last year, they opened up his house and found three grown women in there. One of them

[25]

was his wife, lawfully and legally, though God himself couldn't have said on oath what she was doing there, considering the facts; another woman was his house-keeper, so-called; and the third female in the house was his nurse, also so-called. That's what was on the inside of Stephen Frost's house when he died and when they opened it up.

"God only knows how long the three of them had been living there with him, maybe fifteen-twenty years. His legal wife didn't have anything to say to Stephen about the other two women, because she knew he would kick her out if she objected to his way of living. So she had just stayed there with the other two females, both much younger women, and better-looking, and took what was the share coming to her, which she didn't get any too often. I tell you, men and women in this town are one queer mixed-up lot of people. It's not the foreigners who are doing it; it's always people with names like Emerson and Frost who get mixed up in these things. I might could add more names to that list, if I had a mind to."

"You can leave my name out of it," Ben said, chuckling at Thede. "It couldn't be so today, though fifteen-twenty years ago you could have named me among the rest with ease."

"What about that hired girl at your house, Ben?" somebody said. "Heard that she was going to quit working for your wife and go off to keep house for a younger man."

Ben ducked his head and laughed with the rest of them.

Thede Emerson sat staring at the floor. He neither smiled at what had been said, nor did he acknowledge having heard the name of Emerson mentioned.

CHAPTER III

~~~~~~~~~~~~~~~~~~~~~~~~~~~~~~~~~~~~~~~

THE ROAD TO AUTUMN HILL WAS AN UNIMPROVED LANE
that wound and twisted through the new forest, over
ridges and marshes and hummocky flats, for four miles.
Twice, between Clearwater Village and the Hill, the road
sank into the marshes; twice it shot upward over steep hills
with exposed ledges; and at last it reached the summit,
looping twice around the round Hill before it ended at
the Emerson house.

On each side of the road new-growth pine and birch
stood flush with the narrow winding lane. The way had
at one time been used for pulpwood hauling, and it was
still cut and eroded from the wear. Hardwood boles
had been laid over the marshes; and over the boles, gravel
had been spread. From January to late March the road
was deep in snow, which blew down through the opening
in the forest and made the route impassable except for
horses and sleighs and for men using skis and snowshoes.
In the early spring the streams through the marshes were
high, and water frequently rose over the road. By midsummer, however, the roadbed was dry and firm, and the
heaviest truck could pass over it safely.

For the first two miles on the way to Autumn Hill the country was open. The virgin timber had been cut; the fields cleared of stones, which had been dragged to the sides of the roads and streams to make walls. The forest was continually creeping back to reclaim the farms the moment they were untended, and some of the fields and buildings were already out of sight from the road.

The rest of the distance to Autumn Hill was deep in the forest. White birch, pine, hemlock, and spruce grew so densely that it was difficult walking a hundred yards in either direction from the lane.

Beyond Autumn Hill all the farms had been abandoned. There once had been a road across the hills and flats to Clearwater Corners; but after the townsmen who had lived in that section of the back-country died or moved away, there was no need of continuing the mail route farther than the Emerson home. When the carrier stopped going over the road, the selectmen had ordered it closed beyond Autumn Hill. Since then only a few men had tried to go through to the western end; they had been pulpwood estimators riding on horseback.

The abandoned farms along the road beyond Autumn Hill were now almost entirely covered by the forest. The white paint had peeled from the clapboards of the houses; firs and birches had crept steadily closer year after year until they hid the buildings from sight. There was no one living now between Autumn Hill and Clearwater Corners, a distance of three miles. Once there had been a town grammar school, a Congregationalist church, a rural free delivery route, and homes occupied by eleven families. The winters in the back-country had been more severe than most people could endure in old age, and those who did not die or go mad, moved to other places, usually to nearby villages or to the cities where they attempted to secure year-round employment in paper mills and shoe factories.

Ten years before, the Hopkins homestead, which was situated on the flats a mile west of Autumn Hill, had been one of the largest and finest truck farms in the country. The hayfields had been mown each year, cattle grazed on the hummocky, close-cropped pastures, and the dark loam soil had been broken each spring for the planting of sweet corn, potatoes, shell beans, and green peas.

Then the Hopkins children had grown up and left home to live in the village, in Lewiston, and in Boston. The year after the last son had left home, farming was permanently abandoned. The Hopkins farm was still there; but except for the hand-hewn timbers of the buildings, there was no other evidence of the Hopkins family to be seen. Only pulpwood estimators and deer hunters, had put foot on the place in nearly a decade.

A mile and a half from Autumn Hill, and a short distance beyond the old Hopkins place, was the Edwards farm. The Edwards house, shored-up on all four sides, was still partly standing; it had been built on a solid foundation a hundred and forty years before, and white-lead paint and steel roofs preserved the original wood much longer than most houses had stood without care.

The hot blistering sun of July and August, together with the frost of December and January, had cracked and peeled the paint, and rain had washed the outside boards a dark weather-beaten brown. The roof over the ell had collapsed; the walls that had supported it had fallen upon it. The rest of the house was still standing, except for one corner where the roof had given way under the weight of snow and ice seven years before. The fences and doorsteps, rotted, lay flat on the ground.

Morris Edwards had been the last to leave the homestead. Kate, his wife, died soon after the children had left, and she was buried in the family plot a quarter of a mile away, beyond the potato field, on a pine knoll. Morris had remained there four years after she died, and then he was taken away one forenoon in May to spend the rest of his days in the State Hospital. His mind could not stand the loneliness any longer.

When they found him, he was wandering through the woods in search of the burying ground, which by that time had been covered by the creeping forest. He spoke incoherently to the men who found him, talking in a mumbling voice about things no one could understand. They discovered that he had been living all winter long, possibly for several years, on corn meal and apples. At the side of his bed they found a partly empty sack of yellow meal and a box of rotten McIntosh apples. Within the year after he had been taken to the hospital, he died, and he was buried in a lot that the town of Clearwater paid for in a cemetery near the hospital in Augusta.

That had been the end of the Edwards family, similar in most ways to the end of others. The sons and daughters never returned to the Edwards place, not even in summer, and no one knew where they were living. The town had had to take over the farm when taxes were unpaid;

none of the Edwardses seemed to wish to keep it in his possession.

In the other direction, eastward from Autumn Hill, and nearer the village, the farms were not in nearly so bad a condition. However, all of them between the Hill and the first ridge two miles eastward had been abandoned within the past several years, and they, too, were beginning to be swallowed up by the creeping timber line of birch and pine. The creeping forest was an ever-present menace to cleared fields, to buildings, and to men; it had to be watched, guarded against, and beaten back continually.

There were two dwellings between Autumn Hill and the village. One was occupied by Norah Walton, who lived alone. Norah was between eighty-five and ninety years old, but in spite of her age, and with the help of a small monthly sum from the town's poor fund, she was able to take care of herself. She was given ten dollars a month for food, and out of that she saved enough each year to pay for the cutting, sawing, and hauling of firewood for winter.

The other house was nearer the village. In it lived a French family, the Dussaults, who had brought Dan Randolph's farm. Within the first week after moving in and taking possession, the Dussaults had started to improve the place. By the end of the month, Dussault and his five sons had finished the painting, and had begun the task of clearing the old hayfields of brush and burning the juniper that covered the pastures. They constructed a chicken house with a rodent- and bobcat-proof run, and installed six tie-ups in the dairy barn.

Henri Dussault had very little money at first to spend on the expensive improvements, and he used what he did have left, after having paid Dan Randolph cash for the place, to buy a small dairy herd. Then he reshingled the house and put a steel roof on the barn and fenced a new pasture with woven wire.

From the crest of the ridge, to one looking down at the small, white, porchless buildings in the village and those surrounding them, the country was like a huge green-and-white bowl, at the bottom of which was the glacial lake, its water greener than the grass that grew around it. The smooth green fields around the village, warm and soft in summer, snow-crusted and icy in winter, were dotted with white farmhouses and varicolored stock buildings, protected from the wind and snow by bushy maples and tall elms. Most of the land was used for hayfields and for pastures, but there were squares, like those of an incompleted checkerboard, where corn and potatoes and wheat and oats grew in summer, exposing the black glacial loam.

There were two stores in the village: Ben Robinson's, the oldest and largest, and Frost's. There was a planing mill and a wood-turning plant which manufactured toothpicks and clothespins, both industries formerly owned by the Child's family, but now owned and operated by Napoleon Bouchard. The three largest buildings were the Grange hall and the Baptist and the Catholic churches. The post office was a small wooden building in the center of the village, across the street from the two stores. The other building beside it housed Adelard Lavigne's garage and filling station, and, on the second floor, the telephone exchange. The exchange was operated by Doris Lavallee and her sister, Andrea.

The old families apparently did not care what became of the town; or, if they did care, there was little evidence of their concern. The townsmen were dying faster than they were giving birth to new members. The Franco-Americans, naturalized citizens originally from the Province of Quebec, had begun several years before to move in and take over the best homes in the village; and the Finns, Swedes, Norwegians, Danes, and Russians were buying, and paying for, the most productive and best-located farms in the town. None of the Scandinavians seemed to care how hard and strenuous the labor was on the farms; but as a rule the French seemed to prefer jobs in the wood-turning plants and wood camps to other work that might have been easier.

It was only after the foreign population actually outnumbered the native that any of the townsmen seriously thought of what transformation was taking place in Clearwater. Then, when they woke up one day to find themselves outnumbered and outvoted, Thede Emerson was one of the first to raise his voice in protest. Others soon followed, but all the talking that was done, the threats and curses that were uttered, could not change what had already happened. It was too late then. The townsmen were forced to admit that for every vote they could muster on election day, the French and Scandinavians had two. No native of Clearwater had dreamed of such a thing since the town was first settled a hundred and fifty years before.

CHAPTER IV

JEAN HAD BEEN ASKING HER MOTHER FOR A NEW DRESS FOR more than a year, and ever since she and Frank had become engaged the previous winter she felt that she could not go any longer without some new clothes. Sometime in June, Rosa had, at last, promised to order a dress for her. Thede had never bought anything for her, or given her money; Rosa had supplied what she wished Jean to have, and nothing more. As everyone knew, the money that came into Rosa's hands was spent almost wholly upon herself.

After six weeks of patient waiting for Rosa to get the dress from the mail-order house, Jean was almost hysterical. She ran to the kitchen that morning while Rosa was ironing and pleaded again for it.

"Please, Mama," she begged, "order my dress now. You said nearly two months ago that you would, and you haven't sent for it yet."

Rosa went about her work for several minutes before she said anything.

"How do you know I haven't?" she asked, without looking up from the board. "Maybe I ordered it a week ago, and it hasn't come yet."

"But you didn't take my measurements," Jean said. "You couldn't send for it until you did that, could you?"

"Could if I wished to," Rosa said. "I don't have to run to you every time I do anything. Now stop making me mad, talking about a new dress that you haven't any need of. Save your breath for something dearer."

"But, Mama —"

Rosa's powerful arm lifted the eight-pound flatiron and set it on the range to heat. When she strode across the floor from the table to the range, the muscles of her back rose and fell like those of a woodsman. She was a strong woman, and she was proud of her strength. Even Thede was not so strong as she was, now that he was past sixty and had rheumatism so badly.

"Please order the dress for me now, Mama," Jean said. "I've waited all this time for it. You haven't bought me any new clothes for over a year."

"I thought you had forgotten about that by this time. You don't need a new dress, anyway. Your old ones are good enough for you. Wait and let Gervais buy your clothes for you. He makes enough money hauling wood with that truck of his to support you."

"But you promised, Mama. You said I could have one this summer. And I need one so badly now."

"What if I did? I shall buy it when I get good and ready, and not a minute before. I'm not going to stand for your telling me what to do. Don't forget who I am. You can't boss me."

"But when I'm married, it will be too late. I couldn't ask you for it then. Won't you order it now, so I will have it to wear in the early fall?"

"I'm getting you a few things to be married in; that ought to be enough, and you should be thankful for it. I'm doing enough for you. Let your Frenchman clothe you. It's none of my business."

"But, Mama —"

"You ought to be so ashamed of yourself for marrying a Frenchman that you'd keep out of my sight, instead of coming around all the time to pester me about a dress you haven't any want of. A girl who marries a Frenchman has to take what she can get. I don't wish to see you, nor any of your Canuck kids, either. If Americans aren't good enough for you, then don't come around me. Stay with the French, and don't show yourself here. You'll be jabbering Canuck talk yourself inside of six months, and your children won't be able to say a word I can understand."

"You know Frank speaks just like you and I do," Jean said. "And anyway, even if he did speak French all the time, there would be nothing wrong about it. He can speak both French and English, and I'm proud of him."

Jean began to cry. Whenever Rosa spoke to her like that, she could not keep the tears from welling in her eyes.

"Well, he's a Canuck. That's all I've got to say, and it's enough for anybody to know."

"I love Frank," Jean said. "I don't care what he is. You can say anything about him you wish to, but it won't stop me from loving him and marrying him. I know he is just as good as any of the Frosts and Emersons ever were."

"Don't you mention my family name!" Rosa said threateningly. "You can talk about the Emersons all you care to, but you leave the Frosts out of it. The Frosts were the finest people ever to live in Maine. Those French —"

"The Frosts might have been the finest people once, but they're not the best any longer. I don't call anyone fine who cheats people out of money and commits all kinds of nasty crimes. That's the kind of people the Frosts are now, and you know it."

"Jean Emerson, what are you talking about!" Rosa shouted. "What are you lying about!"

"You know what I'm talking about as well as I do," said Jean, so angry now that she had stopped crying and was looking straight into her mother's face. "I'm talking about those Frosts who live over in Clearwater Corners, and you know it!"

"They are no relations of mine. That family came here from somewhere downstate. My people have always lived in Clearwater."

"What difference does it make where they came from? They have the same name and they call you their cousin, whether you like it or not."

"It's a lie," Rosa said. "I won't listen to you. Shut up! I won't stand to be insulted in my own house by a fresh chit like you."

"You can say anything to me you like and call me all the nasty names you can think of, but nothing bad you say about Frank could be true. He has never done anything like the Frosts have done. Go ahead and talk about him all you like, but if you tell the truth, it will have to be something good and fine. That's the kind of man he is."

"Wouldn't waste my time talking about him," Rosa

said. "I've got other things more important to think about."

Jean held her lips tightly closed to keep from answering her mother. She knew that if she did not restrain herself, she would say things she would later regret.

Rosa went about her ironing, walking stiffly to the range and back, and never looking in Jean's direction.

Half an hour passed in silence while each carefully avoided the other's gaze. Jean looked out the window and Rosa bent industriously over the ironing board. She had almost completed her ironing before she glanced at Jean again, and she was startled when their eyes met.

"You will get me the dress, won't you, Mama?"

"Yes," Rosa said.

"When? Right now?"

"Yes. Bring me the tape measure and the mail-order catalogue from the hall. I left them both there early last evening."

Jean ran to the hall and brought back the tape and the catalogue and placed them on the kitchen table. Rosa folded the ironing board, put away the flatirons, and sat down at the table.

"It would be much nicer if we could have gone to Lewiston and bought the dress there," Jean said. "I like to try clothes on. They fit much better when they are bought that way. But it doesn't really matter now. I'm so happy to get a new dress, I'd almost be willing to take it sight-unseen."

"Turn around in the back," Rosa said. "I haven't the time to waste on running over to Lewiston, or even to the Falls, every month or so. The mail-order garments are every inch as good as anything they have in the stores, and a whole lot cheaper. They overcharge for clothes in the stores, anyway."

"I should like to have the brown one," Jean said, turning the pages until she had found the illustration of the dress she had selected. "This is the one here. Don't you think it's nice-looking, Mama?"

"Brown wool jersey?"

"Yes, that's the one. Isn't it pretty?"

"Well, if that's the one you say you chose, you shan't have it."

"Why, Mama? Why not? What's wrong with it?"

"Because I won't get it, that's why."

"But it doesn't cost any more than some of the others, and it is even cheaper than the other woolen dresses. It's a lot cheaper than the one there on the next page. It costs barely anything."

"It's not the cost I'm talking about now. I know how much I shall spend on it, anyway. You may as well save your breath for something dearer. I won't get it."

"Then, what is the matter, Mama?" Jean said. "I'd rather have a jersey dress like that than any other I've seen this year."

"I've got my reasons why you shan't have it. Now, save your breath for something dearer. My mind is made up."

"But why, Mama?"

"I told you I have my reasons, and they're good enough reasons for me."

"Please tell me."

"If you wore a dress like that, you'd make too much of a good showing to Leland Stokes, that's why. He's got too much of an eye for young girls like you, and I don't want him to have a chance to see you wearing something like that."

"That awful Leland Stokes! I wish he would —"

"Shut your mouth! You have no business talking like that about him."

"He is awful, and you know it, Mama! The things people say about you and him — I'm always so ashamed!"

"You mind your own business and shut up about that!"

"Oh, Mama, why do you do things like that?"

"Are you going to keep this up, or do you care to do anything about a dress?"

Jean covered her face for several moments.

"Mama, please let me have the dress I like. Won't you, this one time?"

"I'll choose what you should have, if you're ready to mind your talk now."

"Please let me have the one I like."

"No."

"But Frank says he thinks the jersey dress would look nice on me. I don't care what anyone else says or thinks about me, anyway, as long as Frank likes me."

"Well! I'm not at all surprised. He would say that, because he's a Canuck. The French girls in this town dress sinfully to my way of thinking, and I shan't allow a foreigner to tell me what to clothe my daughter in. Let him tell his own kind what to wear, but he shan't tell me to dress you like one of his Canuck bitches."

"I think you're real mean to talk like that, Mama. And I wish you wouldn't treat me this way. You know I'd rather have that dress more than anything else I saw in the whole catalogue. It's not true what you said about it, anyway. It's a beautiful dress, and you know it."

"You seem to forget that I'm the one who's ordering the garment, and paying for it with my own money. That's something for you to remember. When your Frenchman pays for your clothes, then will be the time for him to say what he has a mind to, and not when it's my money that's being spent."

Jean gazed hopelessly at her mother. She saw now that Rosa was determined to have her own way, and she was convinced that her mother had taken such a stand against the dress because it was so attractive.

"Then what kind of a dress would you have me wear?" Jean asked.

"That blue worsted. It's stiffer than jersey, and it holds its shape twice as long. That dress will last you seven-eight years. The other one would wear holes in itself before the present year is out."

"But I don't like blue, Mama, and I don't like stiff worsted. Brown is the color that suits me best. I've always worn brown, because it matches my hair and eyes. Blue would look terrible on me, especially blue worsted. I would look awful."

"Told you what dress I would get for you. Now take it, or you get nothing."

"But just think of the other things I would need to wear with a blue worsted dress. I haven't anything to match it. But I do have brown slippers and some brown silk stockings, and my new hat will fit in with it, too. I could never wear my green hat with a blue dress. Even you would laugh at the way I looked, dressed like that."

"Told you to save your breath for something dearer. And I've not the slightest doubt in the world but what that Frenchman of yours would stand up and argue for you, because he would like to have you dress like one of his own kind. Every word that your Frenchman says goes a long way over my head, and you can tell him I said so."

"But Howard said —"

"Well! And what does he have to do with it? That's something I'd like to know."

"I showed him the picture of the dress I wanted, and he said he liked it."

"Go on," she said. "What else?"

"Nothing, Mama."

"I've been wondering about you and Howard for a long time. Why is he always going to your room? What have you and him been doing?"

Jean's face flushed with anger. "Not what you do when you leave the house to meet that awful Leland Stokes!"

Rosa slapped Jean on both sides of her face. "You shut your mouth and mind your own business, and you'll live long enough to have some of your own. When I get ready for you to meddle in my private life, I'll give you plenty of notice. Now, shut up!"

Rosa raised her hand as if to strike her again, but Jean shrank aside.

"One of these days I'm going to catch Howard in your room, and then we'll see what kind of a pretty little speech you can make."

Jean sat down in the chair beside the table and began to cry. She could not keep from crying then and she covered her face with her hands. Rosa watched her for several moments; then suddenly Rosa walked to the table and shook her roughly.

"How do you know what I do?" she demanded. "Who's been telling you?"

"Everybody knows it," Jean said, without looking up. "Why shouldn't they? They talk about you all over town every time you go out to meet him. I can see you slip out of the house when you think no one notices you. Papa sees you, and Howard, too."

"Well, I've got the right to meet Leland Stokes, or anybody else in town, if I wish to. Now, haven't I? Say so! Haven't I the right?"

"I don't know," Jean murmured.

"You know I have! Nobody is going to tell me what to do and what not to do. I'll be my own boss, and nobody else shall!"

"But it isn't nice, Mama. If you've got to go on like that, get a divorce, or do something. It's vulgar now, and you should know it."

"You go out evenings with that Frenchman of yours, don't you? Well, suppose I should say that isn't nice? What would you say to that?"

"But Frank and I are going to be married and, besides, we don't go around in the woods. We go to dances and to shows, and to places like that when we go out. And you are married to Papa, too."

"There's no difference. It's all the same."

"No, it isn't. Papa —"

"What has that old pile of skin and bones got to do with it, with me, or with anything else under the sun?

[43]

I have lived with him in this house for twenty years, and I have yet to have any trouble with him about what I choose to do. Who would do his housework for him? Who would have scalded his milk cans for him ten years ago? Nobody, unless she was getting good pay for doing it."

"Why did you marry him then? You don't love him now, and haven't enough respect for him to stay in the house at night. You take advantage of him just because he's old."

"I would have been a fool not to have married him when I had the chance. Yes, just look at all that money he has — two hundred thousand of it! He'll be dying before I will, thirty-forty years sooner, and I'll get my share, and a good share at that. You haven't any need of it, anyway. I ought to take yours. You won't be in the family any more — marrying a Frenchman. Not in my family, anyway. That's how I am going to have it if I have my way."

"Then it's true, what Howard said!"

"What did Howard say?"

"He said you were waiting for Papa to die so you could marry Leland Stokes, and get all the money, too. Howard said that you were hoping that Papa would die right away."

"Shut your nasty mouth!" Rosa said, moving quickly toward Jean. "It's a God damn lie!"

She raised her hand as if to strike her daughter, but Jean sank back in the chair and began sobbing again. She felt certain now that her mother hated her.

"You quit meddling in my private life after this — and you can tell Howard that, too."

"Mama, there's something wrong with us — with all of us. I know there is, and you do, too. It's in us, and we can't help it. I don't know what it is — I wish I could get away from it. But I can't. It must be something in our family — we're just like all the other old families in town. It's going to ruin all of us. Sometimes I think it would be better if all of us were dead. Then all the awful things would have to stop happening."

"Go on and say whatever you like about yourself, and it'll probably be true. But you can leave me out of it. You don't have to tell me what to do. If what I do is a sin, then it's my sin. My personal affairs are none of your concern. That's something you'd better remember hereafter, too."

There was silence after that. Rosa waited impatiently, expecting Jean to accuse her further.

"Well!" Rosa said at last. "Is that all you have to say? Are you going to keep your mouth shut about me from now on?"

"Yes, Mama," she replied.

Jean went to the couch and fell upon it. She tried not to cry any more, but she could not help it.

While her daughter's face was turned toward the wall, Rosa picked up the tape measure. After a glance at Jean, she made several quick calculations. When the figures had been set down on the order blank, she sealed the letter and stamped it.

"Get up and stop your crying and take this letter to

[45]

the mailbox before the carrier passes," she said, standing over Jean. "Get up, I said, and act like a grown-up person for once. That's enough of your babyish crying."

Jean took the letter without looking at her mother and ran out of the kitchen. By the time she had placed it in the box and put up the flag, she felt better for having cried such a long time. She walked back along the path to the kitchen, wondering if Rosa could ever be happy with anyone, or anyone happy with her.

Rosa had taken several baking pans from the rack behind the range and had begun getting dinner ready to cook when Jean got back.

"It's all settled now," Jean said, trying to smile. "We won't have to talk about anything like that again. But there's one thing I would like to ask about. It's about —"

"Howard?"

"Yes."

"I know exactly what you are going to say, but go ahead and say it anyway."

"What is he going to do about going off to college this fall?"

"Howard will be doing what he's been doing, or, rather, what he ought to be doing now. He's working on the town roads, but when fall comes, he's got to stay at home and do the chores. I can't do them, and your father is getting too old."

"But, Mama, if Howard doesn't go off to take his engineering course this fall — if he has to stay here — aren't you afraid —"

"Afraid of what? I'm not afraid of anything. What are you trying to talk about, anyway?"

"You know as well as I do that he doesn't want to stay here."

"Do I know it! Have I heard anything else for the past six months?"

"Can't you — won't you persuade Papa to let him go? Please try to, Mama!"

"Have told you about the chores that must be done on this farm twice a day the year 'round. Howard has got to do them, starting this fall. He ought to be here now."

"But Howard — the way he feels about it — he might —"

"Do what — run away from home?"

Jean said nothing. She was afraid she was going to cry again if Rosa began abusing Howard.

"Well, let him run away from home if he has a mind to," Rosa said. "Wish he would. We can get a hired man to do the chores, and then when the time comes to settle the estate, we won't have to divide it up with him. A hired man never shares in his employer's estate, no matter how hard he works, unless it's a bequest in the will, and I don't guess Thede Emerson has lost his mind yet."

"How can you talk like that about Howard, Mama?" Jean said. "Don't you love him at all?"

"Guess I like him, all right, but money is money, and it's hard to get, the world over. It's hard to get your hands on, and after you get it the best thing you can do is hold on to it with tooth and nail. When you get to be as old as I am, and have lived with milk cans as long as I have, you'll think so, too."

"I'll never think that way as long as I live. If I ever get to be hardhearted and stingy, I hope I may never live another day."

"Young people all talk like that for a while, but they soon grow up to know better. I've heard it said before, but after thirty-forty years of hard winters in these back-country hills you learn some sense about money."

"I don't care anything about your talk of money. I'd like to know what you and Papa are going to do about Howard. Can't you see that if you try to make him stay here this winter, after he's been planning for all these years to study civil engineering, he might do something terrible?"

"Well, he won't need my leave to go away from home if he has a mind to. That's what I've got to say about it. We can employ a hired man for the chores. It'll be less bother that way, too. And cheaper, in the long run. Sure, tell him to go on off, if he has a mind to."

"It's not that, Mama. Howard — oh, what's the use of talking about it any more! Papa doesn't understand, and doesn't wish to, and you wouldn't understand if you were told."

Rosa leaned forward, gripping Jean's shoulder.

"The way you beg for Howard sounds to me like you've got a peculiar interest in him. Have you been sleeping in bed with him? Is that what's been going on upstairs between you two?"

"Oh!" Jean cried. "I may be an Emerson and a Frost, but at least I'm not like the rest of you!"

"I'm not so sure, young woman," Rosa said slowly. She laughed shortly to herself. "You will have a hard time proving to me that you're so saintly — after this."

CHAPTER V

~~~~~~

THE DOOR OF JEAN'S ROOM WAS CLOSED WHEN HOWARD
stopped at the top of the stairway and, instead of going
straight to his own room, he stood there in the darkness
of the hall staring at the bright streak of light that was
shining through the crack over the threshold. He was
certain that his sister was in her room, but after waiting
for several minutes he still could hear no sound on the
other side of the door.

"Jean," he called in a low voice as he tiptoed closer
to the door.

He waited nervously in the dark hall for her to answer
him. There was no sound anywhere in the house. Thede
and Rosa were in the living room downstairs, and neither
of them was talking.

"Jean," he said again, and then he knocked lightly on
her door. "Jean — are you in there?"

The door was suddenly opened and she was standing
before him. He went as far as the threshold and stopped.
His sister watched him questioningly.

[49]

"Where have you been, Howard?" she asked after several moments.

He was about to answer her, but before he could say anything, she was speaking again.

"Why didn't you come home for supper tonight?" she was asking him with an anxious expression. "I saved something for you in the kitchen. Your supper's still warm. Wouldn't you like to have it now?"

"I don't care for any supper tonight."

Jean took several steps backward and he followed her into the brightly lighted room.

"What's the matter, Howard?" she asked tensely. "Please tell me what it is."

He went to the open window, still not answering her, and stood looking out into the night.

"I wish you'd tell me what's the matter, Howard," she urged her brother.

He turned quickly away from the window and walked back to the middle of the room.

"Something is the matter," she said, going to the door and closing it. Then she came back across the room and sat down on the bed in front of him. "Something happened, Howard. I knew something was wrong the moment I saw you. Please tell me what it is, Howard. I want to know."

"Papa hasn't any right to tell me I can't do what I want to," he spoke out angrily. "I'm old enough to know what I want."

"What did Papa say?"

"Well, he hasn't said anything lately. It's the way he looks at me every time I come into the house. He won't let me forget. I know what he's thinking every time I see him. He's saying that I've got to stay here and do what he says."

She waited patiently for him to finish telling her everything he wanted to say.

"The reason I didn't come home for supper tonight was because I was sitting out there on the stone wall thinking about everything. And the longer I think about it, the more I want to leave home this fall. Going away to study is the only thing that matters now."

He suddenly sat down in the rocking chair in front of her and stared at the bare wall behind her.

"Papa can't stop you, Howard," she said encouragingly, "if you make up your mind to go to college this fall. He hasn't any right to keep you from doing that."

"I wish I could feel that way about it," he admitted. "But I can't. I can't break his grip on me. He doesn't have to lock me up, or do anything like that. All he has to do is say he won't let me leave. I can't do anything as long as he's got that grip on me. I don't know what's wrong with me."

Jean got up and stood in front of him.

He tried not to look at her, but he could not take his eyes from her. She was standing only a few feet away and he knew he would have to get up from the chair in order to keep from looking at her then. She continued to look directly at him, and after another moment he got to his feet.

He realized that he had come to Jean's room with the intention of talking to his sister about his trouble with their father, and he knew that he should not say anything about Frank Gervais. Each time he saw Jean he could not keep from trying to think of some way to let her know that he wanted her to change her mind about marrying Frank or anybody else. But Frank was going to marry her, and he knew he would have hated any man who was going to take her away. Now, as he stood there and looked at Jean, he hoped that something would happen — that anything would come about that would prevent his sister from marrying and going to another house to live.

Jean turned and looked away from him. She stared at the closed door, not daring to let him see her face then. She wished she could tell Howard what she was thinking, but she was afraid.

Still not looking directly at him, she went back to the bed and sat down.

"Jean —" Howard said in a trembling voice.

She closed her eyes to keep herself from looking at him now. While she sat there on the side of the bed wondering what she should do, she heard somebody coming up the stairway. Then the door of her room was opened, and Rosa stood there looking first at her and then at Howard.

"Mama — what do you want?" Jean asked fearfully.

Rosa came slowly into the room, walking noiselessly over the brown carpet. She came as far as the foot of the bed. Jean had not moved.

"Well!" Rosa said with a triumphant smile on her lips. "What's going on in here between you two?"

Howard turned quickly, startled by his mother's voice.

When he saw the expression on her face, he turned away from her, fearful of what she might say.

"There's no use trying to fool me," Rosa said to both of them. She nodded her head knowingly. "You can stop thinking that right now."

"Mama —" Jean began.

Rosa ignored her and looked directly at Howard.

"You didn't come home in time for supper this evening," Rosa said to him, "but you managed to get here in time to come into her room, didn't you? I suspected I'd find something like this going on up here. I should have been watching for it a lot sooner. What have you been doing up here?"

Neither Howard nor Jean answered her.

"Well, what were you doing, Howard?" Rosa said persistently. "Speak up — say something!"

Howard glanced at her, but said nothing.

"Can't you speak up? What's wrong with you?"

"What do you want me to say? I haven't been doing anything. Can't you see I'm not?"

"I can see you're not doing anything right this minute. I'm not blind. But what I'm asking is what have you been doing? What are you doing in her room?"

"Please don't keep this up, Mama," Jean pleaded. "You mustn't, Mama!"

Moving quickly, Rosa reached forward and pulled Jean's dress above her waist.

"At least you've got all your clothes on," Rosa said, turning and walking away from her.

"We've been talking, Mama," Jean told her.

"About what?"

Howard stood up. "I'm going to bed," he said. "Good night."

Rosa walked between Howard and the doorway. He waited in the middle of the room and made no effort to move past her. No one spoke for several moments.

Presently, smirking a little, Rosa said, "So you've been talking, have you? Well, what were you talking about? Speak up!"

"What difference does it make?" Howard said, angered. "You've said what you wanted to say, haven't you?"

"It's about time you spoke up," she said, laughing at him. "And you can get so mad at me that the top of your head flies off, young man, but you won't be able to fool me for one split second. I know what you were doing in here. I can tell what's been going on. You were going to get into bed with her, weren't you? Don't lie to me! She's been trying to get you to do that, hasn't she? I'm not blind, even if I don't know everything that goes on. I know all about it, young man. If I had come up here a little later, I'd have caught you and her in bed together, wouldn't I? I didn't this time, but I will. One of these times I'm going to catch you at it. What'll you have to say then?"

Jean, sobbing, fell across the bed.

"It's a lie!" Howard shouted at his mother.

"So you're talking at last, aren't you?" she said, laughing at him.

"You know it's not true!"

"That's enough out of you! Now, shut up!"

"Then you stop saying things like that!"

Rosa went forward several steps and struck his face

time after time with the palm of her hand. At first, Howard did not move, and she continued slapping him until he ran to the corner of the room in order to escape from her. Rosa followed him, but she did not hit him after he had put his arms over his face.

"Maybe that'll teach you a lesson," she told him as she turned and walked back across the room to Jean.

Jean moved backward, frightened by her mother's threatening manner.

"Now, go to bed," Rosa commanded. "I don't care what you do after that Frenchman gets you, but I'm going to see to it that you don't get pregnant in this house until he takes you away. I'm going to watch you every minute, inside the house and out. I'll slap you silly if you don't obey me. Now, you keep Howard out of this room. And stay away from Leland Stokes, too. If you let Leland Stokes talk you into going to the woods with him, I'll shoot you both. I mean that. I wouldn't hesitate one minute, if I found out you'd done that."

While Rosa was on the other side of the room, Howard ran out and went to his own room. He could not hear what was said after that, but after a while the slamming of Jean's door jarred the house and then he could hear his mother's footsteps as she went down the stairway to the hall below. For a long time afterward he lay awake listening to the sobbing of his sister.

CHAPTER VI

~~~~~~

FRANK GERVAIS DROVE OUT TO AUTUMN HILL ON FRIDAY
evening to take Jean to a dance in the village. It was
the first time they had been together in almost a week.

Before Jean could tell him of what had happened
between Rosa and herself several days earlier, Frank
began telling her of his fear that something might happen to prevent the wedding from taking place as they
had planned. Somebody had told Frank, either jestingly
or in earnest, that Thede Emerson would surely change
his mind before the wedding could take place and forbid
him to see Jean again. Frank had not taken it seriously
at the time, but the more he thought about it, realizing
Thede's prejudice against his family, the more uneasy
he had become.

Frank, like almost everyone else in the town, knew
that Jean's father had done something strangely unlike
himself when he gave his consent to their marriage.
Almost everyone believed that Thede would change his
mind when the time actually came for his only daughter
to marry a second-generation French Canadian. The
people who doubted his final consent and approval could

not understand how a man who had spoken out so violently against anyone of foreign birth or extraction would permit his only daughter to marry and live with a man whose parents were Canadian-born French from the Province of Quebec.

When Frank began talking about his apprehension, Jean tried to reassure him that nothing was going to happen that would prevent their marriage. She knew her father well enough to know that he really wanted them to marry so he would be relieved of the expense of supporting her. Thede was now so anxious for her to marry that he had asked her several times that summer to set an earlier date for the wedding. Each time he had spoken of it, she had told him that both she and Frank thought it best to wait for the original date in October.

"I've been told that some people are saying your father's going to change his mind at the last minute and make you marry somebody with a name like his," Frank told her. "Somebody with a name like Hopkins or Walton or Gordon."

"Don't pay any attention to the gossip, Frank," she said. "The townspeople are always looking for something or somebody to talk about, and we are a good topic of conversation because everyone in Clearwater knows how Papa feels about you and your family. He doesn't feel that way because of you, but because you don't have a name like Emerson or Frost. And Papa isn't going to change his mind now. He's counted on it so much now that he'd make me marry even if I told him I wanted to wait a while longer. And even if he said I couldn't marry you, there'd be nothing to stop us from going somewhere else to get married. You'll stop worrying now, won't you? Papa is so glad that I'm to be married that he has already invited everybody in Clearwater to the wedding."

They were driving over the road to the village and had reached Norah Walton's aging, dilapidated, shored-up house. A feeble yellow light from an oil lamp shone through one of the windows of the kitchen. Jean hoped she would be able to see a glimpse of Norah Walton, because whenever she saw Norah, it made her intensely happy to be engaged to Frank. Norah, it was said, had never married because she had refused, when she was a young girl, to marry the man chosen for her by her parents; she had been in love with a Norwegian woodsman and, in order to prevent their marriage, her father had killed him.

Although Jean watched closely, they drove past the dwelling without seeing Norah.

"All that talk had me worried," Frank said after a while. "You know how some people do — they tell you something to make you uneasy, and then if you halfway believe it, they swear they're telling the truth. I generally know when somebody is joking, but this is so serious I forgot, and believed every word of it. I won't the next time, though, because if anybody in the town knows your father, it's you, Jean. I don't understand him any more than he understands me, but after we've been married I'll probably be able to understand Americans the way you do. I don't believe Thede even tries to understand me or any of my people. Sometimes it looks to me as if he doesn't wish to. My mother and father say that most of the Old Americans in the town feel that way. They can't seem to see anything good in any of us. They call us foreigners and treat us like we have no right to be here. We're like most people, except for our names and that we haven't lived in America as long as families like yours."

"I think that's one reason I want so much to marry you, Frank."

"Why, Jean? What do you mean?"

"Because my parents feel the way they do — and I don't want to be like them. I don't want to be an Emerson or a Frost or a Walton. Something terrible would be sure to happen. I'm afraid sometimes that I'm going to do something I know I shouldn't."

"Do what, Jean? I don't understand."

"Let's not talk about it any more, Frank," she begged. "It frightens me — to think that I might — I don't know what! But it's something deep in me — and in Howard, too! Please, Frank! Don't make me talk about it. We're going to be married in October— aren't we, Frank? Please say we will!"

"Of course, Jean," he assured her. "You mustn't worry like this."

"And if anybody tries to stop us, we'll run away and be married somewhere else, won't we? Please say we will!"

"We'll go to Quebec. Your father couldn't stop us after we got there."

"That would be lots of fun, Frank, driving up to Quebec to be married. I'm beginning to wish now that Papa does try to stop us. That would be a wonderful honeymoon, in Quebec!"

Frank said nothing else. He had wished to go there in the first place, but they had decided that they needed the money to help pay for the farm and furniture. Furthermore, their house would require painting in two or three years, and they had to save for that. There were so many things to be bought to start housekeeping, and so much more required for the operation of a farm, that every dollar counted.

After they had reached the village and had entered the Grange hall, Jean remembered that she had not told Frank all that Rosa had said.

Couples were dancing all around them as they entered the door, and they joined in at once. While the orchestra played, Jean had time to tell him about the dress. When she had finished telling him, they circled the floor once before he said anything.

"You won't have to put up with her much longer, Jean. I wish we could go ahead and marry now, so you wouldn't have to stay in that house another day. I don't like to talk about your mother, but I can't help saying that I think she's the worst mother I've ever heard of. You deserved somebody better than she is. If my mother had done what Rosa has, and had said to me what she says to you, I would have run away from home long before now. I couldn't have stood it."

The orchestra stopped suddenly, and the dancers went to the seats along the walls of the building to wait for the next number.

"This is going to be a Boston Fancy," Frank said. "We'd better find some seats and sit down where we can watch the dance better."

The orchestra, which was composed of a pianist, a violinist, and a trombone player, began one of the numbers for the square dance. All the elderly people jumped up at once to join in. Without hesitation, they squared off and began going through the movements of the Boston Fancy. Age did not keep them from enjoying themselves; the older men and women present were skipping over the waxed floor with more agility and enthusiasm than some of the younger ones.

While it lasted, Jean and Frank sat on a bench against the wall and watched the older men and women enjoying themselves. There were seventy or eighty people in the hall then and more were arriving. None of the summer-people were seen, because the dance was not open to the public. Members of the Grange invited those whom they wished there, and outsiders were not welcomed.

Next there was a round dance, but Jean and Frank kept their seats and watched. Over and over again the orchestra played the only two musical selections they used during the evening for the modern dances and then later, as a novelty, the musicians played a new number. There was applause for the unfamiliar music. Whenever the orchestra played "The Stein Song," every man and woman present applauded for an encore. Everyone, young and old, liked to hear and dance to the music of "The Stein Song"; it was almost as popular as "Pop Goes the Weasel."

Over in a corner, partly hidden by the evergreen decorations, Jean saw Ben Robinson dancing with the Robinsons' hired girl, Flora Randolph, while Ben's wife, who had stopped dancing a dozen years before, sat alone on the other side of the hall and watched disapprovingly. Ben did not seem to be concerned about the many frowns

[61]

she gave him, because he whirled Flora around and around, kicking his heels behind him and acting as if he were nearer twenty years of age than seventy. After a while Ben's wife pretended that she was not watching him any longer, but when Ben held Flora close to him, she could no longer sit still and bear it. As soon as the orchestra finished the number, she beckoned to Ben with her finger, trying to attract his attention and to make him leave Flora. Concentrating delightedly on his dancing, Ben succeeded in evading her frowns and finger-crooking.

"I'll bet Ben Robinson gets a talking to when he goes home tonight," Frank said. "If Flora wasn't such a good-looking girl, his wife wouldn't care what he did, but she can't stand to see him dancing with Flora and looking so pleased about it. They always manage to dance together several times whenever there's a dance in the Grange hall. Ben steps around to her bidding when he's at home, but Mrs. Robinson can't manage him when he's outside the house."

After a Lady-of-the-Lake, Jean and Frank joined in the next waltz. Everyone who was coming that evening had got there by that time and the floor was crowded. Ben had Flora in his arms again, and this time they were careful to keep well out of Mrs. Robinson's beckoning range.

At eleven o'clock most of the older people had begun to leave, and soon afterward only the younger ones were left to dance. There were no more square dances, and the orchestra began playing its two selections without interruption. Soon nearly everyone, including Jean and

Frank, was whistling or singing "Good Night, Sweet-heart" and "The Stein Song."

Axel Nordenskjold asked Jean for a dance, and while they were on the floor, Frank saw Fredda Knudsen and her sister Daga. He danced with each of them once and then went off looking for Jean. He saw her for a moment, but he lost her in the crowd before the music started again, and when he saw her next, she was dancing with one of the Henata boys. After that he began looking for Sonya Vyssotsky, whom he had seen earlier in the evening. Sonya had been the first girl he had ever taken to a dance, and when he found her and reminded her of it, she left her partner and danced the next three numbers with Frank.

During the next intermission Frank went to the refreshment stand and bought two dishes of ice cream and searched until he found Jean. After eating the ice cream, Jean said she was ready to go home.

They left the Grange hall and started home shortly before midnight. On the way to Autumn Hill, Frank drove slowly. Neither of them had anything to say until they reached the bridge over the stream near Norah Walton's house. Norah's light was out, and she was probably asleep; but a car had stopped at the bridge ahead of them and several men were standing beside it. While Frank drove past, several whose voices he recognized called and invited them to stop, but they drove on.

"What are they doing at that bridge so late at night?" Jean asked, looking back at the men beside the automobile. "Why did they ask us to stop?"

"They're beer drinkers finishing up their bottles," he

told her. "It's getting so late I didn't think we'd want to stop. Besides, they sometimes get a little noisy at this time of night."

"Since I'm not much of a beer drinker, I don't guess I would like it," she said. "But why are they out on our road so late at night?"

"Those beer drinkers hide their bottles under every bridge in town," he said. "Every time there's a dance in the village, they cache their bottles along the roads and come out for a few drinks during intermission. They get together and go from one bridge to the next until the last bottle in town has been emptied."

"How do you know so much about it, Frank?" she asked, pretending to be stern.

"I went along with them — before I found you," he said.

"How do I know you won't go out at night like that again? I mean, after we're married."

"I'll be satisfied to stay at home," he said, kissing her. "Don't you worry about that."

Nothing more was said for a long time, because by then they were within half a mile of Autumn Hill, and Jean realized that she might not see Frank again for several days. He never stayed at the Emerson house very long when he brought her home like that at night. Rosa had a habit of raising a window and shouting angrily at him to go away and let her sleep. Even when they made no noise, Rosa rarely failed to watch for the headlights of Frank's car and to order him away from the house the minute he came to the doorstep.

"You won't believe what people say after this, will you, Frank?" Jean asked in a whisper, holding his hand tighter.

"I'll try not to," he told her.

"Please don't, Frank. Nothing is going to happen. I won't let anything happen."

"All right, Jean. I won't pay any attention to it the next time I hear it. As long as I know you mean that, I can laugh at any such talk after this."

"And I do mean it, Frank," she assured him. "Nothing can keep us from living together now, anyway. Neither Papa, nor Mama, nor anything in the world. As long as I have you, I'm not afraid of them. But don't ever stop loving me, Frank. I've got to have you. If it weren't for you, I would be afraid — awfully afraid."

"Afraid of what, Jean?"

"Nothing," she said quickly. "But please don't stop loving me — I'm so afraid without you!"

After they had got out of the car in front of the house and had started walking slowly toward it, Jean saw somebody sitting on the doorstep. She held tightly to Frank's arm.

They went forward cautiously, and when they were several yards away, Frank recognized Howard. Jean saw him at almost the same time.

"What are you doing out here so late, Howard?" Jean said, sitting down beside him. "Are you sick? What's the matter?"

Howard looked up and smiled at her. He motioned to Frank to sit down beside them.

"Nothing much," he said casually.

"But it's after midnight already, and you have to get up at five to go to work. You'll never be able to wake up in the morning if you don't hurry and go to sleep."

"I'll wake up, all right," he said. "The alarm clock wakes me up every morning. It hasn't failed yet."

"You're still working on the roads, aren't you, Howard?" Frank asked. "You haven't stopped yet, have you?"

"I'm still working. I never fail to put in a full day, unless it's raining. The only ones I've missed this summer have been wet and rainy ones, and I always go over there every day in case we might be able to work, no matter how hard it is raining. If it weren't for the wet and rainy days, I'd be a rich man by now. But one or two days lost every week cuts down the pay check. There's nothing I can do about the rain, though."

"Why are you talking like that, Howard?" Jean asked him. "What's the matter?"

"Not a thing," he said.

Jean had been looking at him all the time he was talking to Frank. She still did not know what had made him stay up so late, because usually he went to bed by nine o'clock.

"Why don't you go to bed, Howard?" she asked him again, insistently.

"I'm not sleepy. But I am going to bed in a few minutes, anyway."

"Then why don't you go to bed now? It will kill you to stay up half the night like this and then get up at five in the morning to work all day."

"I'm going," he said. "Don't lecture me about it. I just

didn't feel like going to bed and sleeping. That's all the trouble was."

"You're not worrying about this winter, are you?"

"A little, I guess."

All three of them sat staring out into the darkness. Frank had been watching first one and then the other until they stopped talking.

"What are we going to do about it?" Jean asked, reaching for Frank's hand. "Howard has got to go away to school."

"I don't know," he said. "I wish I knew of something we could do about it. It'll be a shame if Thede doesn't give in. I know how it is. I wanted to go to the university, but my family couldn't afford it. That's why I stayed home. I had to help them. But it's different with Howard. Your father has the money."

"Something has got to be done," Jean said. "I can't stand seeing things go on like this. We've got to make Papa let Howard go. If he doesn't go this fall, he may never go."

Howard stood up between them, smiling down at Jean. He turned around and looked at Frank for a moment.

"I'll do something about it. It's not your place to worry about me. I'll fix things up some way. That's why I haven't been able to sleep much at night lately. I lie awake trying to think of some way to fix things. I've thought of several, but none of them seems to have much promise of working out right. I'll have to think a little harder from now on."

He laughed and, turning abruptly, went through the door into the house. Frank and Jean watched him until he was out of sight.

"Good night," he said, his voice coming out to them from somewhere in the hall. "I'll see you again some wet and rainy day."

Jean had begun to cry before the sound of his words had left her ears. She leaned against Frank's shoulder and held her hands over her face.

"I know how badly you feel, Jean," he said, trying to comfort her. "It's pretty bad, but maybe something will happen between now and the time for him to leave. There is some way of helping him to go away to school, if we can think of it before it's too late."

"Oh, I just know nothing will, Frank. That's what makes me feel so badly all the time. That's why I can't keep from crying every time I see Howard and hear him talk about going off to college. Something tells me that he never will."

"It's not all that hopeless, Jean. He'll make it, all right. If Thede Emerson has all the money that people say he has, then there's a pretty good chance for Howard to get what he needs. My mother and father used to say they couldn't afford to let me have certain things and do certain things, but someway they always gave them to me sooner or later. That was because they didn't have much money and had to wait until they did have it."

"But that's different. Your mother and father love you. Papa doesn't —"

She began to cry again, so loud that Frank was afraid that she would wake up Thede or Rosa.

"You're driving me off, Jean," he whispered, kissing her. "You'll wake them up in another minute."

"I'm sorry, Frank," she said, holding him tightly. "I

[68]

tried not to cry, but I just can't help it when I think of Howard. He's the only one of my family I could possibly cry over, and I feel so bad whenever I think what may happen to him. Sometimes I'm afraid something awful will happen."

As she spoke, a window was raised somewhere. Frank hastily kissed her and ran out across the lawn towards his car.

"*Bon soir, ma plus chère*," he said to Jean. "*Je te verrai à bientôt. Il me faut aller à moins que cette salle cochonne-là ouvrisse sa gueule, peut-être qu'elle jette sur moi la chambre. Je m'en fiche de ses affaires après Octobre.*"

Rosa leaned out the window, trying to see what was taking place. Before she could curse at Frank, he had started his car and was turning it around and driving off in the direction of the village.

CHAPTER VII

When the foreman blew his whistle at twelve-thirty for the dinner hour, Howard propped his shovel against the nearest tree and walked to his lunch box where he had left it with his coat that morning. They were building a stone-base gravel-top road over the marsh on the way to Warsaw Lakes that week. Already most of the stones had been laid, and two more days' work would finish the road.

The other workmen were beginning to eat dinner, most of them leaning back in the shade against the stone wall that separated Sam Burton's farm from the right-of-way. Sam had been out in his field all that morning cultivating his vegetables and pulling grass and weeds out of the soil. Even though it was twelve-thirty, Sam was still working. Fifteen minutes later he would stop work and go to the house for his dinner. He always worked a quarter of an hour longer and began that much earlier than anyone else, no matter what it was he was doing.

Howard reached his lunch box and found a place under one of the elms beside the road. Just as he began eating

[70]

his lunch, Lin Childs sat down nearby. Lin chewed bites of his roast-beef sandwich for several minutes before he spoke.

"Guess you heard about all the fuss-and-feathers at our house last night," he said to Howard then, and picked up another beef sandwich and took several bites from it. "It was a mighty big to-do for so late in the evening."

"What happened?" Howard asked. "I didn't hear about anything, Lin."

Howard waited while Lin chewed some more, wondering if Lin were joking with him.

"No fooling," Lin said after a while. "There was plenty of fuss-and-feathers. The old man shot a redskin through the foot with his moose rifle last night."

Howard laughed, certain then that Lin was joking about something.

"Maybe you don't believe me, Howard, but it's the truth. My old man did shoot an Indian."

"What Indian?"

"One who used to live on the reservation at Oldtown."

"What was he doing? Selling woven reed baskets?"

"No. He wasn't that kind of Indian. This was a different kind of redskin. He looks just like any Indian, except that he wears better clothes than most people. And he's a teacher, too. He's a college professor."

"Was it the Indian who's been having dates with Evelyn?" Howard asked. "Is that the one your father shot?"

"That's him," Lin said. "The old man drew a bead on him just as he was coming through the gate at our house last night and stopped him right there and then. He was starting to go into the house with Evelyn. The old man said grandpa had died fighting redskins 'way out in Montana, and that he was going to keep it up till there was none left in the whole country. My old man doesn't think much of Indians."

Evelyn Childs, Lin's sister, had been having dates with the Indian that summer. She had a job in a summer hotel at Warsaw Lakes, ten miles away, and she had met him there soon after she started to work. She had always come home for a visit on Sunday afternoons, and each time she came she had brought the Indian with her.

"Evelyn didn't like it at all when the old man plugged him in the foot," Lin said.

"What did she do?"

"She almost had a fit. I never saw her take on like that before about anything. She and the Indian had just got married."

"Married?" Howard said. "She married the Indian?"

"Sure. Really married. Yesterday morning she and the Indian left Warsaw Lakes in his automobile and drove over to New Hampshire and got married. The old man heard about it, and so he went to the village to swear out a warrant against the Indian. My old man was sure mad about it."

"What kind of a warrant?" Howard asked. "What kind of a warrant could he swear out against the Indian?"

"A white-slave warrant. He said he was going to have the Indian arrested and put in jail for violating the white-slave act. He said there're plenty of laws to keep anybody with a brown skin from marrying a white girl, and that he was going to use every inch of the laws. He's got a lawyer-friend in Augusta who tells him all sorts of things about the law and how to sue people and how to get people arrested."

"But if they really got married in New Hampshire," Howard said, "the Indian couldn't be arrested for anything. That lets him out, doesn't it? He can get married anywhere he wants to even if he is an Indian, can't he? It looks to me like your father waited too long to do anything about it."

"That lets the Indian out, all right," Lin said, "and that's what made the old man so mad about it that he took down the moose gun and waited for them to come back. Just when they were walking through the gate, the old man bore down and shot the Indian in the foot. He had been waiting for them all day, sitting cramped on a stool by the front door."

"Did he say anything to them before he shot?"

"Sure. And that's when they said they had been over to New Hampshire so they could get married right away. Evelyn said that if they tried to get married here, the old man would've done almost anything to stop them. Guess he might have shot the Indian a little higher up if he couldn't have stopped it any other way. He says Indians are foreigners just like the French and hunkies and ought to be run out of the State of Maine."

Lin was busy eating then and had no more time to talk about Evelyn and the Indian. Evelyn was a year or two older than Howard, but he had known her ever since they started to school together in the first grade. While she was growing up, she had said she was not going to be the kind of girl who stayed at home all her life waiting for somebody to marry her, and then end up becoming a bed-warming housekeeper on a back-road farm for somebody named Frost or Watkins or Morris who was too stingy to marry and support a wife and family. She had said that two of her aunts had become bed-warming housekeepers on back roads and that before she became somebody's woman in the house she would rather wash dishes in Boston or Portland for the rest of her life. When Evelyn finished high school, she got a job at one of the summer hotels in the next town, and that winter she began studying stenography at home. In the spring of the following year she found a good-paying job in a large hotel at Warsaw Lakes. That was where she had met the Indian.

The Indian she had married had been born on the reservation at Oldtown. Howard had seen him frequently during the past two or three summers when he was driving through the town in his automobile on his way to Warsaw Lakes or to Boston for the week end. His name was Roger Western. Howard had always thought until then that all Indians were named John, because all the ones he had ever seen were called by that name. Most of the Indians he knew wove reed and willow baskets and closet hampers during the winter months and sold them from door to door during the summer. But Roger Western was not that kind of Indian, Howard soon discovered. He was a professor at a college in Ohio, and he had a degree of doctor of philosophy. During the summer he was employed as a tutor at the hotel at Warsaw Lakes. Evelyn had said that Roger had written several books on the subject of anthropology, and that he had studied for two years at one of the universities in Europe.

After hearing that, Howard knew that Roger Western was no ordinary Indian and, besides, that he was much better educated than anybody else in Clearwater. Roger's face was unusually wide, his hair was very black, and his skin was the color of weather-worn brickwork, but he dressed in the same kind of clothes other people at the hotel at Warsaw Lakes wore, and he talked just like anyone else did.

Evelyn's father had taken a dislike to Roger Western the first time he came to the house with her. Evelyn had brought Roger to Clearwater one Sunday afternoon, and that was when John Childs shut and locked the door to keep him out when he tried to follow Evelyn into the house. When Evelyn's father had done that, she turned and walked out. As she was leaving, she told her father that if Roger Western could not come into the house, neither would she.

There had been considerable talk for a month after that happened, and most of the townsmen had sided with John Childs. They had said that Roger Western might be all that was claimed for him, that he might even be a college professor somewhere in the West, but just the same he was an Indian. Few townsmen had ever seen an Indian other than the ones who traveled through the state from door to door selling woven reed baskets, and Roger Western had to be treated like the rest of them. Howard had heard Thede swearing and shouting about Roger Western when the Indian first began having dates with Evelyn. Thede had said then that no Indian could ever come into his house, and that as long as he lived he would do his best to drive them out of the State of Maine, just as he had been after the French and Scandinavians for a lifetime.

"It's going to be the ruination of us," Thede had said angrily, "this thing of foreigners of all breeds taking up with our native women the way they do. We'll end up being measly-part Americans and part God knows what else. If there's no law against it, there ought to be. If this keeps up like it's been going, people like us won't find any native American women left, and we'll be forced to take to the foreign females. It's a shame that Americans like us here in Clearwater have to bed foreign females for the sake of having a woman in the house."

Howard had felt sorry for Evelyn then, because he knew that when two men such as Thede Emerson and John Childs took such a stand, there was very little hope of her being able to overcome their prejudice.

Lin slammed the top of his lunch box and found his cigarettes and matches. He offered Howard a cigarette and struck a match for the light. Howard closed his lunch box and stretched out on the deep grass.

Over in the adjoining field, Sam Burton had placed his hoe against the stone wall and had started walking to his house for noonday meal. Propping up his head slightly, Howard watched Sam cross the garden plot. Sam was not so old in appearance as most of the elderly townsmen, although he said he was well past sixty. He still walked erectly, his back was not stooped, and he could do as much work as any able-bodied man in the town. He made his living by raising green peas and sweet corn and selling the produce to the hotels at Warsaw Lakes during the summer season. Every spring he was the first in town to get his land broken and peas planted. He always managed to be first, by ten days or two weeks, to have green peas for sale. He raised sweet corn for market, too, but even if he had been unable to find a market for it, he would have felt amply rewarded in having the distinction of being the one who raised the first sweet corn of the season.

Every time Howard saw Sam Burton he could not keep from watching him as he moved about in his garden. For among those who knew him well, Sam was conceded to be the oddest man in Clearwater. Not since Howard could remember had he ever seen Sam Burton when he was not wearing his stiff white collar and green four-in-hand tie. The collar was celluloid, and he owned only one, but he never left the house without it. In the hottest part of summer, when the thermometer went above ninety in the shade, Sam could always be seen somewhere around his farm working as though he did not know what heat was. And the high white collar would be around his neck, cramping his Adam's apple and binding his throat. But he never took it off while he was outside the house. Even if he was hoeing peas and a storm came up, Sam would remain in his field through the hardest downpour, wearing his high white collar and green tie. Each day he wore a different shirt with the celluloid collar. Sometimes it would be a white one; more frequently it was a shirt of black- and red-striped madras. His shirts were always spotless, just as clean as his collar, which he rubbed with a damp cloth twice a day, noon and evening.

Sam Burton never perspired while he worked in his

truck plot; Sam drank a secret preparation of his own that closed the pores in his skin. Other men sometimes drank prepared water for the same purpose, but no concoction was so effective as Sam's, and he steadfastly refused to give away his secret formula. People had become accustomed to thinking of Sam Burton as the man who wore a high white celluloid collar and who never perspired; even the fame he had won as a truck farmer — being the first man in town each spring to have green peas ready for picking and sale — was not greater than that. Other farmers occasionally raised peas that were as green and sweet and large as Sam Burton's, and ears of sweet corn that were as well filled out, but none of them had ever been able to work all day during the hottest part of July and August while wearing a high white celluloid collar and not perspire to some extent.

"Why've you been watching Sam Burton all this time?" Lin asked, turning over and gazing across the stone wall.

"I've been wondering who's going to inherit Sam's farm and buildings when he dies," Howard said. "Everybody says Sam has no kin. What'll become of his property?"

"Sam's taken care of that. He's deeded his farm and buildings to the town. He did that four or five years ago so he wouldn't have to pay taxes on them. Now the town has to let him live on his farm rent-free and tax-free, and besides that the town has to keep up the insurance on the house and barn. Sam's no fool. He knew what he was doing when he deeded his property to the town."

Sam disappeared from the scrutiny of watching eyes when he opened the kitchen door and went inside to eat his noonday meal. The meal was already prepared, and he did not have to wait until he could build a fire in the range to cook it. He always cooked his dinner at the same hour he ate breakfast so that he would not have to waste any time during the noon hour. He only rested a little while then, as he worked fifteen minutes longer than other people, and started back to work fifteen minutes earlier. He gave the impression of working longer, but actually he worked only as long as anyone else. The rest of the farmers stopped work at five in the afternoon, the same hour that the road workers quit for the day, but Sam Burton always stopped promptly at four-thirty. Even during the planting and harvesting seasons, when every hour of daylight was valuable, Sam stopped at four-thirty in the afternoon; if there were two or three weeks of harvest ahead of him, he stopped every day on the minute of half past four. But Sam did as much work as anybody else, if not a great deal more, because he worked ten hours a day, seven days a week, rain or shine, during the eight open months of the year. The other four months he rested in his house and read the year's accumulation of newspapers and magazines.

'What time is it?" Lin asked.

Howard took out his watch. It was exactly one o'clock.

"We've got another half hour yet," Lin said. "But if we were working for Sam Burton, I'll bet he wouldn't give it to us."

Howard stretched out on his back and gazed up into the cloudless blue sky. He closed his eyes momentarily but promptly opened them again. He knew he would drop off to sleep if he allowed himself to close his eyes, and then he would have waked up at one-thirty sleepy for the rest of the day.

"Say, Howard," Lin called to him, "have you noticed how people are marrying foreigners these days? They're marrying all kind of foreigners — Canucks, squareheads, Indians, and all sorts of queer fish. I wonder why that is? Even your sister is doing it, or getting ready to. Frank Gervais is all right, though. I've never held anything against him. But why are so many people marrying foreigners? There must be a good reason for it."

"I don't know," Howard answered. "I don't know why my sister wants to get married to anybody. She wouldn't have to. But nobody can talk her out of it now."

"Maybe it's because the foreigners are a little bit different from us," Lin said. "I've been thinking that maybe I'd like to try it myself, before much longer. Most of the foreign girls are really good-looking, and I know for a fact that they can really treat you good when they want to. After dating some of them, you sort of get spoiled, I guess it is. I've had dates with some of them who could make you feel like a million dollars. That's something that makes you stop and think. Why don't you look around, Howard, and pick yourself out a good-looking one?"

"I don't care about getting married — not to anybody."

Lin looked at him closely for several moments, but Howard said nothing more.

"Guess maybe I'll see if I can get another date with one of those Hedenstjerna girls tomorrow night," Lin said. "They are the best-looking girls in town, not even except-ing the French ones. Both of them are particular about giving dates, but I think I can talk myself into one. I had a date once with the youngest one and I've been wanting to go back again ever since. She sure was cozy and nice."

They lay looking up at the blue sky for a long time.

"Don't you want a date, Howard?" Lin asked after a while. "Why don't you make one with the other Hedenstjerna girl? She's about a year younger than you."

Howard shook his head. "I don't care about it," he said.

"That's funny," Lin remarked. "You don't have dates with any girls, do you? Why not?"

He shook his head again, but made no reply. Lin turned on his side and watched Howard thoughtfully.

"Say," he said presently, "maybe that's why you don't want your sister to get married. I never thought of that before. That could be the reason, couldn't it?"

Howard still did not answer his questioning, and presently Lin sat up and looked around. Sam Burton had already come back to his truck garden, and he had been at work for the past several minutes.

Lin groaning, got to his feet. He lit another cigarette and walked around stretching his legs. Howard lay where he was, glad of every minute of rest he could have. It was hard work shoveling gravel, whether in the pit or on the road. His back and arms were much stronger then than they had been three months earlier, and his muscles were never sore any more, but the hard labor tired him. Most of the men who were working on the road had been doing physical labor such as that all their adult lives, but he was twenty years younger than most of them and he was not accustomed to it.

"Wish you could have seen that Indian last night when the old man plugged him in the foot with the moose gun," Lin said, laughing to himself again. "It was the funniest sight I ever saw. That Indian sat right down on the ground and stayed there looking like a scared doe in the brush before she starts to run. He just sat there watching the old man until Evelyn ran back and fell all over him to keep the old man from shooting him again. Guess he would have done it, too, if she hadn't got between them. The old man was the maddest I've ever seen him. He's never had any use for Indians, anyway. He says their woven baskets don't last any longer than a paper bag in a thundershower, and hold only half as much to start with. Guess if he had his way he'd shoot all the redskins he could locate. I don't know who thinks less of the foreigners — your old man or mine. But there's one thing for sure. It's that people like them will always agree on hating the Canucks, squareheads, Indians, and hunkies."

Howard sat up. The starting whistle was blowing. He got up slowly and walked behind Lin until he reached his shovel. Without waiting until the others began work, he dug the blade of the shovel deep into the pile of gravel.

CHAPTER VIII

JEAN WAS SITTING IN HER BEDROOM ON THE SECOND FLOOR when she heard Howard on the front doorstep calling her. Before she could run to her door to answer, she heard him down in the hall calling again.

"Here I am, up here," she said, running to the stairhead and looking down at him. "What is it?"

"A surprise," he said, holding something behind his back. "You're supposed to guess what it is. Can you?"

"What are you doing at home this time of day, Howard? Why aren't you working?"

He turned and looked out the front door, nodding his head in that direction.

"Don't you know? It's raining today. I had to come home after working an hour and a half — all free labor for the town."

"I thought it looked like it would rain early today, but I didn't know it had started. I've been up here cleaning since breakfast."

"Time's almost up already. Aren't you going to make even one guess? Try it."

"Please tell me what it is, Howard," she begged, running down the stairs. "Don't tease me so much. Is it really mine?"

He held out the flat paperboard box.

She reached for it, not yet suspecting what was on the inside.

"The new dress that you've been waiting two weeks for. It came in the mail this morning."

"Not two weeks — two years," she said.

"Well, anyway, here it is now."

"How do you know it is the dress for me?"

"Because it looks like it. Nothing else could be in a box like this, unless it were a couple of shirts, and nobody I know would order shirts for me. Open it up and let's see what it looks like."

All at once, with the box in her arms, Jean remembered. Slowly she unfastened the twine and tore off the strips of glued paper from the edges. In the white paperboard box was a dress; she knew there was a dress inside, but she did not open it.

She looked at it for several minutes before she allowed herself to touch it again.

"What's the matter?" Howard asked her. "Don't you like it? I thought you said that was what you would like to have most of all right now. There's a dance at the Grange hall next week, you know. You would like to wear it then, wouldn't you?"

"It is not the dress I asked for. Mama said I shouldn't have a jersey dress."

"Well, go ahead and open it up and let's see what it looks like."

Jean tore at the tissue paper that was around the garment and shook it open, holding it up in front of her. When the dress came unfolded in her hands, she could scarcely believe her eyes.

"It's exactly the one I wished!" she cried excitedly. "Mama did get the one I asked for, after all! She must have changed her mind about what she said to me, because she told me that I shouldn't have it, and we even got into a fight over it."

"Are you sure it's the right one?" he said gravely. "You'd better look at it carefully. You know Mama."

"Oh, I'm sure! I'm positive! It's exactly like the one in the catalogue. Something must have happened to Mama — she may have ordered it by mistake, though. Something must be wrong, somewhere."

"Well, you're not going to send it back, if she did make a mistake, are you?"

"Not if I can help it. I don't know what she's going to say about it, though. She might drop dead when she finds out this one came, the one I wished all the time."

"It looks good to me," Howard said, "but you look fine in anything."

"Wait until I go upstairs and try it on, Howard. Please wait, and then tell me how you think it looks on me. I'll be gone only a minute."

"All right, I'll wait on the doorstep for you."

Jean picked up the dress, folding it carefully over her arm, and ran up the stairs to her room. After she had laid it out on the bed, she stood a moment and looked at it before starting to take off the cotton dress she was wearing.

In another moment she was jerking at her dress and

pushing it from her waist to the floor. She had barely stepped out of the old one before she was lifting the new brown jersey over her head and shoulders. It was, after all, exactly the same dress she asked for. The material was light brown jersey, and the collar was trimmed with white-and-orange diagonally striped flannel. The cuffs were trimmed with the same material, with an added band of black between the white and orange. She could hardly wait to see herself in the mirror.

Before she could walk across the room, though, she had pulled the dress around her waist and down below her knees. The moment she saw herself in the mirror she knew something was wrong. There was something about the dress that caused it to bulge on her body. She did not have to look at herself the second time to find out what the trouble was. The realization came to her with startling clarity, and she was angry with herself for not having thought of it when she first opened the box and saw the dress.

Now, when she looked at it again, she knew that Rosa had still had her own way about the dress. She had changed the measurements to fit herself, and had ordered it in that size. The dress was several inches too large for her all over. The waist could be gathered in her hands and folded almost halfway around her again, and the bust was almost as large as that. The dress hung on her in such folds that it looked plainly as though it had been made for someone twice her size. Rosa was that large, and the dress would undoubtedly fit her as well as any possibly could. It was certainly Rosa's dress.

Jean jerked the frock from her body and threw it with

all her might against the door. When it fell there, she stood looking at it while her lips trembled uncontrollably.

Tears suddenly filled her eyes and she could no longer see the dress in a heap on the floor.

"Why does Mama treat me this way!" she sobbed. "Dear God, please don't ever let me hurt anybody the way she does me!"

Somewhere in the rear of the house, out near the old stock barn, Jean could hear her father talking in his loud thin voice to a strange man. Probably it was someone who had come to Autumn Hill for the purpose of selling Thede lightning rods. There were always agents and salesmen knocking on the door and asking for Thede. People everywhere knew that her father had a lot of money now, and he was usually the first that agents called upon in Clearwater. But Thede never bought anything from them. If he were not busy at the time, he allowed them to present their sales appeal, and then he would say he did not wish to buy anything and would walk away, locking and barring the door to the house and feeling pleased that he had the sense to protect himself and his money no matter how enticing a salesman's wares might be or how entreating his plea.

This time the agent, who said he was from Boston, had been selling a new brand of paint that was guaranteed to outlast and outspread any other paint yet perfected, but Thede had cut him so short that the salesman had hastily stuffed his literature back into his pockets without bothering to replace it in his salesman's case and had left.

Thede was cross with himself for having cut the sales-man off so abruptly. He had nothing else to do and he knew that he had deprived himself of a half hour's, maybe an hour's, entertainment looking over all the salesman's samples and wares, but paint was something that Thede did not want to talk about — for Autumn Hill was begin-ning to show indications of neglect for the first time since it had been built.

It has once been a magnificent place. There were traces of its earlier splendor in the scattered evidences of former care; but nothing now could hide from the eyes of the most casual visitor the scars of unrepaired door-steps and putty-cracked window sashes. And when once a house in Clearwater became dilapidated, the heat of summer and the frost of winter hastened its decay and inevitable collapse.

Although Thede Emerson had never considered it, the decline of the farm and buildings was in keeping with the traditions of his life. The farm and house at Autumn Hill had served his purpose, which had been to make as much money for himself as he possibly could, regardless of the welfare of his family.

Now that he had achieved his ambition to his complete satisfaction, he had no desire to go to the expense of pre-serving the buildings from decay. He had taken from the farm what he wished; his children could have what was left, and, if they had the ability, try to duplicate his success. Although nothing at this period of his life could have persuaded him to leave Autumn Hill for Jean and Howard in the condition in which he had inherited it, a deep and lasting impression had been left upon him by the statements he had heard made in Robinson's store to the effect that all of them were tired old Americans whose only hope of family survival was the introduction of new and virile blood into coming generations. Secretly, he realized that something had to be done if Emersons of Clearwater were to continue living on the earth. War-making invaders, at other times elsewhere, had often furnished invigorating blood for such families; consequently, he had given his consent to a peaceful invasion of foreign blood into his family so that his own lineage would survive and flourish long after he was dead.

There had been many times in recent years when Thede, driving out of the woods at the marsh, had viewed Autumn Hill from a distance and had realized what had happened to the homestead. However, he never permitted himself to look at the farm and buildings for long from such a perspective; he feared a weakening of his determination.

The house on the Hill was a century and a half old. It was two stories and a half, and in it were fourteen rooms, not counting the attic which had been unused for nearly fifty years.

Thede Emerson had not painted the house in seven years; and it was beginning to need paint badly, although the gleam of white lead that remained from former coats was superficially intact. Here and there, however, where the structure was most exposed to the sun and rain, cracked and peeled boards gave warning that the wood beneath could not be preserved forever without aid. Paint, and paint alone, would keep the house standing. There were too many shored-up and fallen-down houses on abandoned farms nearby, almost within sight, to reckon otherwise. Thede knew that.

He had been watching the paint for a year or more. He was waiting, day by day, for the final moment of grace. He did not wish to go to the expense of painting when it could be delayed for a time. He was not conscious that it was his dogged determination to save a month's, or even a year's, time that was hastening the eventual collapse of the building. But water seeping through the cracks in the roof and under the sun-warped clapboards would rot the sills and beams that held the structure upright. Nothing could be more certain. Thede would have been the first to order the painting and roof repair done had he believed that it was actually needed. He had become blind to many things during the past ten years.

Autumn Hill had been named for its October color. The first Emerson in Clearwater, John Howard, who had penetrated the forest and built his home, and who had afterward returned to Newburyport for his family, had been captivated by the beauty of the early fall in that section of the Commonwealth of Massachusetts which later became the State of Maine. He had built the house and barns, felling pine and hardwood from the hillsides, sawing, hewing, and planing the lumber with his own hands. Then he began the task of clearing the land for crops and pasture. He had named the farm Autumn Hill long before the buildings were completed. They were not ready for occupancy until three years after the first excavation for the cellar had been made.

Autumn Hill had always been one of the finest farms in Maine, and Thede Emerson had, by his labor and industry, made it into perhaps the best at the time. For almost forty years he worked at it, getting up at three o'clock in summer, at five in winter, to work long after dark by lantern light. He had added to his dairy herd year after year, breeding, improving, and caring for the stock until his cows had produced milk, cream, and butter of the richness he had thought they should. The bulls he owned were valued at many thousands of dollars, and the milch cows had all been pure-blooded and protected animals. And while he was devoting his life and energy to the production of milk, he was at the same time adding to his herd of beef cattle. There never had been a time when he believed that any other stockman or dairyman could match the animals at Autumn Hill, and few men had ever questioned his boasts. Autumn Hill was the ideal of hundreds of small cattle owners who came to see it, and who went away vowing to build up a similar farm on their own land.

Six years before, after nearly forty years of labor, Thede had sold his herd of milch cows, his beef cattle, his bulls, his horses, and his sheep, and had banked the money. Now he was drawing interest on more than two hundred thousand dollars invested for him by the trust department of his bank. He was a rich man in Clearwater; for a time he was regarded by all who knew him or who had heard of him, as the richest man in that section of the state. Thede was proud of his success, and he was even prouder to say that he was a wealthy man. But now when a man mentioned Thede Emerson's name, usually the first thought that occurred to anyone was about Thede's private life. His wife, Rosa, cared more for the company of other men than she did for his.

"Thede Emerson made a lot of money for himself, but he never calculated to spend it on his wife and family," one man said. "He married her to have her scald milk cans. When she found out that Thede never intended to love her, she began to let anybody love her and that went on for years until by the time she was thirty-five she was as common as a woman gets, and it was all Thede's fault to begin with. He expected her to scald milk cans the rest of her life for him. She's not to blame. Thede Emerson's the one to blame for the way Rosa's acted. And if his children hate him, and won't live with him after they're of age, he has only himself to take to account. Children don't hate their mothers and fathers unless they're driven to it."

There were many other things said about Thede. But the real Thede Emerson was the man who had driven himself to make a lot of money, who had whipped his children into subservience and had spent the emotional vitality of his wife until she had nothing left but greed and malice and wanton revenge.

But from the moment he sold his cattle, Thede lost all interest in the appearance of the farm. When the money was banked, he took the position that Autumn Hill would have to get along the best it could without help from him. There was no resemblance now between the Autumn Hill of the present and the Autumn Hill of ten, twenty, or thirty years ago. It had all the indications of a farm about to be abandoned.

Juniper was beginning to choke out the grass in the pastures; wild blackberry briars were covering the crop land; the old hayfields were already shoulder-high with gray birch; and white pine seedings grew in every available opening. A stranger would have hesitated to believe that the farm had once been given expert cultivation and care. Only the house, cow tie-ups, and hay barn showed that once the farm had been worth coming a hundred miles to see.

But Thede was not worried about the present-day appearance of Autumn Hill, nor did he regret that it no longer looked as it once had. He now had his interest to compute, his bank statements to check, and his bond coupons to collect. He did not have to worry about the price of whole milk delivered in Boston, or about quotations for beef on the hoof. He was well satisfied with things as they were, and proud of his wealth, even if there was nothing left at Autumn Hill to show for his years of labor. He was nearing seventy now, and if he should live to be a hundred, he would still have the two hundred thousand dollars, and more besides, to live for. The original sum was accumulating interest every day, and the longer he lived, the more he would have in the bank.

Thede worried about Howard, however. His son expected him to furnish the money for a college education, and nothing Thede had said so far had discouraged Howard and convinced him that there would be no money for an engineering course in Boston. Every time the matter was mentioned, Thede had said flatly that he was not going to give Howard a dime of his money, but Howard continued to believe that he would be able to leave home in the fall.

Jean, too, had caused him to worry for several months. That was when she told her father that she wished to marry Frank Gervais. For nearly a year Thede would not listen to her, and then gradually he began to relent and, after all those months, he finally gave his consent. His reasoning then was that he would still have Rosa in the house to do a woman's chores and that he would be relieved of the expense of supporting his daughter.

The more Thede thought about it, the more pleased he was with himself for having come to that decision. He was able then to realize that Jean would be better off as the wife of a self-supporting Frenchman than she would be as the wife of a Walton or a Hopkins. He had become convinced that it would be to his advantage, economically, to have her marry anybody except one of his own kind. What little faith he had left in the virtue of his own kind was becoming increasingly meager and insignificant.

CHAPTER IX

~~~~~~

AFTER LABOR DAY, WHEN PRACTICALLY ALL THE BOYS' AND girls' camps and the summer houses had been closed for the season, Clearwater became normal again. There were no large automobiles to speed over the gravel roads at seventy and eighty miles an hour endangering life and property and frightening men and women out of their wits. It was the time of year when the townsmen began to come out of their homes for the first time since spring and to look around to see what the country was like following the two months' carnival.

Throughout September there was a general feeling of relief. A man could walk along a highroad to the village and feel that his life and limbs were safe. Or he could drive his horse and wagon there and not be compelled to go all the way to the stores and home again with two wheels and his horse's feet in the ditch. When the boys' and girls' camps closed and when the summer-people went back home, Clearwater began living its own life again.

On the other hand, there were many men, more especially those with something to sell to the summer-people, who had been glad to have so many visitors during the two-month season. Butter could be sold at the door for eighty-five, ninety cents, or even a dollar a pound, and sweet butter for sometimes as much as a dollar and a half a pound, while during the other two months of the year there was the weekly trouble of packing and shipping it to Boston to be sold wholesale at a lower price. Even then it took the check a week to arrive. Eggs also brought correspondingly high prices, and occasionally a barrel of potatoes could be sold for several times what the market had offered the fall before. Green peas and shell beans were always in demand, and the price they brought was enough to require several trips a week to the banks in Augusta and Lewiston for deposit.

In the village stores men talked more freely in September, now that there were no strangers to overhear. In July and August a man had to be careful what he said, because summer-people from New York and Philadelphia would more than likely be within hearing distance.

During the month of September, and on into October, the townsmen really enjoyed living. There was no close damp heat to make the middays muggy, winter was still several weeks away, and the cool air brought renewed life and energy to everyone who breathed it. After the harvest had been gathered, there was little to do but to enjoy life for a while.

Later, in November, the hunting season would open. Deer were always plentiful. By starting out early in the morning a man could walk through the woods and brush a short distance, possibly a mile or two, and within an hour he would more than likely find a buck or doe to bring down with rifle fire.

When the deer season opened each year, Thede had always sent Howard off to bring back a kill for meat. For the past four years Howard had brought in a buck or doe for Thede, but this year there seemed little chance of his being there to go hunting. Howard knew that if he worked through the month of September he would not have the time because, when November came, he expected to be at the engineering school in Boston.

The Saturday before the final week of September had long been in Howard's mind as the time when he would take some definite action about going to Boston. He had already given the construction superintendent notice that he would stop working that day, and he had asked for his full pay at that time. He wished to forget the road job so that he would have nothing else on his mind when he tried for the last time to get his father's consent.

He had no trouble in getting paid the full amount due him. When five o'clock came, he put on his coat, jumped on a gravel truck, and started for Autumn Hill. The truck was going only half the distance there, so he had to walk the remaining two miles. He did not mind that. He walked as fast as he could, running along the flats and down the hills.

When at last he got to the house, he was breathless, but so excited that he did not stop to think how tired he was. He had given up his job on the road, collected the pay due him, and he was now ready to carry out the hardest part of his plans.

First of all he went upstairs to his room and took a bath. Then he put on clean clothes and went down to the dining room and ate supper alone. Rosa had finished washing the dishes and she and Thede were sitting in the next room, their shoes besides their chairs, resting. It was yet too early to light the lamps, as there was twilight still in the room.

Howard could hear Jean upstairs, moving trunks and opening closet doors and dresser drawers. He knew that she was packing her clothes, getting ready to leave home. She and Frank were going to leave the day after the wedding. Thede and Rosa had insisted that they spend the first night at Autumn Hill in order that the wedding and the celebration, which would be equally as important to them as the ceremony, would not be cut short by their leaving before the guests did. Many people were coming to attend the wedding ceremony and to take part in the celebration.

Before he pushed back his chair from the table, Howard heard Thede get up, walk across the carpeted floor in his socks, and light a lamp. Howard waited at the table, thinking over his plan of action. He wished to be sure that he had his argument well in hand before he started talking to Thede. For, after once beginning, there would be no time to stop and think of what to say next; Thede would probably wish to talk just as much as he did.

The tension he had been under all day made Howard nervous, and now that the time had come, the moment when he would gain everything or lose everything, he hesitated. He had made most of his preparations for going away, but he knew that the hardest part of all, securing

Thede's consent, was still before him. After getting his father's approval, packing his clothes and getting ready to leave would take only a few minutes.

But securing Thede's consent, now that the time had arrived when he had to attempt to get it, seemed to be more impossible than ever. He thought of all the times when Thede had said that he would never allow him to leave home, and he recalled how often his father had cursed him for talking about it so much.

"It's this time, or never," he said under his breath, trying to find courage in the words. "And it's got to be this time. It is the only time that matters. I will make him say I can go. I've got to make him say it!"

He turned and looked through the open door into the next room. Thede had begun reading the paper, and he could see Rosa's stockinged feet on the other side of the table. He did not know why he should think so, but for some reason he believed he would not fail this time.

He jumped up, pushing the chair away behind him, and walked with determination through the door into the next room. There was not a sound, not even the rustle of Thede's paper, not even the squeak of Rosa's chair, anywhere in the house. From where he was he could not even hear Jean upstairs.

Thede glanced over the top of his newspaper, but he did not look at Howard for more than a moment. He went back to reading the column as though Howard had not entered the room.

Rosa began rocking in her chair then, waiting to see what Howard was going to do. She knew by the way he stood in the center of the room that he was getting ready to say something again to Thede about going off from home.

"I quit work today," Howard stated, waiting to see what effect the words would have on Thede.

Thede lowered his paper a few inches, just enough to permit him to look Howard full in the face. However, Howard noticed, his father did not lower the paper to his knees as one would who was about to begin a conversation.

"Learned your lesson, did you?" Thede said.

"What lesson?"

He tried to keep control of himself so that Thede would not be able to confuse him. He knew that once his father got the better of him, he was lost. It would be impossible to start all over again after that.

"Young boys have to find out such things for themselves."

"What things?" Howard said.

He hoped that as long as he questioned Thede in that manner, Thede would not be able to abash him. Usually, Thede was able to stop him before he could tell his father what he wished to say.

"You can make more money working for yourself than you can by digging gravel for other men."

Howard bit his lips, trying to think of something to say that would cause his father to change his manner.

"Thirty dollars a week is a good wage to receive for learning a lesson," Thede said.

Just then Howard thought Thede was going to close the conversation and begin reading again. But instead, Thede leaned forward.

"How much money have you got now?" Thede asked.

Howard tossed his bankbook on the table at his father's side.

"I've saved three hundred dollars," he said. "I need five hundred more."

The moment the words were out of his mouth he realized that he should not have mentioned the five hundred until later. But the words had been uttered; he would have to risk starting from there.

Thede picked up the savings book and glanced at the pages. Weekly entries averaging twenty-five dollars had been made on two entire pages of the booklet. There was a total of a little more than three hundred dollars after the last entry.

"How did you come to spend that four — five dollars a week you kept out?" Thede said. "You don't need to spend that much money a week. Why didn't you bank thirty a week? That's what you were making, wasn't it?"

Howard deliberately ignored the questions. He had already made the mistake of saying too soon that he wished his father to give him five hundred dollars. He realized now that he should have waited a little longer before saying that. In the silence of the room each man waited for the other to speak first.

Rosa rocked faster, smiling to herself. Thede looked across the room at her for a brief moment, and then he lowered his eyes again to the figures in the bankbook.

Howard was beginning to fear that his father had disconcerted him again, and while he was trying to think of what he should do next, Thede began talking.

"You can settle your debt by drawing this three hundred dollars from the savings bank and paying it over to me. After you've paid me for your board and keep all these years, I might be willing to talk about loaning you three hundred dollars. And I charge eight per cent, payable twelve times a year on the day the interest is due me. If you kept up your payments on the three hundred dollars, I might be persuaded to listen to you about a loan of five hundred dollars. And it would still be eight per cent interest for that, too."

"I'm not asking you for a loan now," Howard said quickly. "What I'm asking for is what you owe me."

"Owe you!" Thede shouted, jumping to the edge of the chair. "Now, what in God's name would I be doing owing you money? Tell me that!"

"I've got to have an education, and you ought to see that I get it. I've worked for you on this farm for twelve years, day and night. I've cultivated the garden, done chores, milked cows, fed horses, plowed, harvested, and done everything else that you told me to do. And I did all of it without ever getting a cent of pay. Now I'd like to collect five hundred dollars of what is due me. Are you going to pay me what you owe me?"

"Not while I've got the voice to say — *No!*"

Jean walked into the room, taking a seat near the door. She had heard Thede and Howard through the walls of the house, and she had come down to take up for her brother and to plead for him if necessary. She knew by the tone of his voice that this was the time when Howard was going to make a final effort to get Thede's consent to let him go to Boston.

When he saw Thede lean back in his chair and reach

for the newspaper, Howard suddenly realized that if he did not say something soon he would not be given a chance to talk any more. When Thede had heard all he cared to hear, he had a habit of forbidding anyone to talk. Howard knew that he must say something to his father while he still had the opportunity.

"Now, look here, Papa," he said, stepping closer to the table. "I've been waiting a year for you to say I could go to college this fall. There's no more time left. Classes start next week. I'll have to leave Monday in order to get there in time. I've got to have the money. I've got to! I have three hundred dollars saved up, and you must let me have the other five hundred. Tuition and textbooks and board will cost all of that for a year. I'll pay you back as soon as I am able to. I'll pay you back every cent I borrow if you tell me to, with eight per cent interest — your eight per cent. I've got to have the money this time, Papa. I've got to have it!"

Thede chuckled to himself, leaning back in his chair to take a good look at Howard.

"So that's what's on your mind, is it? Five hundred dollars! Do you know what you are talking about — talking like five hundred dollars was five pennies? By God, five hundred dollars brings me in forty dollars a year in interest. You couldn't pay interest on it, even if you did have security to put up."

He laughed again, louder than before.

"I said I need five hundred dollars — with eight per cent interest, if you won't let me have it any other way. I'll find a way to pay you your forty dollars' interest. I'll pay every cent of it."

Rosa slowly stopped rocking her chair and leaned forward to hear what was going to be said next.

"Well, if you want some advice, I'd say you'd better go back and try to get your job on the road before somebody else takes it. You'll need to hold that job a long time if you aim to get any more money. And that's the only way you'll ever get it."

"I've already made up my mind about what I'm going to do," Howard told his father. "I want that five hundred dollars."

"Do you think you can tell me what I'm going to do, or are you going to listen to what I tell you? Answer that!"

Howard could feel the strength of his father's will confounding him.

"I tell you I need the money, Papa —"

"Well, hear this then! Here's one thing you should pay heed to. I'll see you in hell before you get a penny of my money! Did you hear that?"

Howard nodded slowly.

"And I want that three hundred dollars you've got, too," Thede said. "That'll help pay me back some of the money you owe me for your support all these years. Now, make up your mind to pay me what you owe me."

Howard had become desperate. He knew that he could not stand in his father's presence much longer without becoming subjected to his will.

"Damn you!" Howard shouted loudly. "Give me that money!"

CHAPTER X

~~~~~~~~~~~~~~~~~~~~~~~~~~~~~~~~~~~~~~~

BOTH THEDE AND HOWARD WERE SO ANGRY THAT THEY could not speak plainly. Thede's face was fiery red, and Howard's hands trembled no matter how hard he clenched his fists and bit his lips to control himself.

"You'd better be saving your wind for road work, and for doing chores. When you are ready to listen to me, I'll tell you something else, too."

"I know what you are going to say, so what's the use of my trying to keep you from saying it. I know exactly what you will say."

"If you know so well what I'm going to say before I say it, then where is the use in asking me?"

"But Papa, I've got to have the money. I'll do anything you tell me, if you will let me have it. It would be different if you were poor, but you've got the money, and a lot more besides. I've got to go to Boston. I can't —"

"I've got a job for you," Thede said. "You won't have to go back to work on the town roads. I've had this job for you a long time, and I guess you know what it is."

"I don't care what it is. I'm not staying here."

"Well, you're going to care, because you're going to

stay right here at Autumn Hill. It'll require a lot of your time and attention, this job I've got laid out for you."

"I've already told you what I'm going to do. I'm leaving here Monday morning."

"Let me tell you something, young man. You're going to stay at Autumn Hill for the rest of your life and do the chores that are waiting to be done. That's what you'll be doing the coming Monday, and every day from then on. I've got pride in my family name, and you're going to stay at Autumn Hill and keep up the Emerson pride when I'm gone. I've made up my mind about that, and nothing's going to change it. I didn't raise you to be an expense to me, either. You've got to earn your board and clothing. I've spent considerable money on you for nineteen years. That three hundred dollars you have in the savings bank will help pay some of it back. You owe me a lot of money."

"Then it's about time you found out that you can't make me do what you tell me," Howard asserted. "And I don't believe you can do anything about it, either. I'm old enough now to have some rights. I haven't got to stay here, and I'm not going to stay here this winter and do chores for you or anybody else. I'm going to leave Monday morning. Now, what are you going to do about it?"

"Not going to do a blamed thing but sit back and see to it that you do the chores and other work in a thorough-paced fashion. I've got that to see to."

Howard suddenly felt so weak that he did not know how he was to continue standing any longer, or how to move himself to a chair where he could sit down. He felt as though something had treacherously drained his strength and bound his muscles. Even his brain was powerless to force movement into his limbs.

Jean came closer to Thede, stopping at the table where she bent over it.

"Papa, can't you see what you will be doing to Howard if you force him to stay here? You mustn't do that for anything. You mustn't, Papa. Please listen to him. You must listen to him and let him go."

"And you can shut up, too!" Thede said, glaring at her. "Nobody said anything to you. Keep your mouth out of this. You'll be sorry if you don't keep it out. I'll see to that."

Howard had remained standing as long as he could, and now he felt that the sooner the thing was over with the better off he would be. He had never felt so despondent. He did not see any use in pleading or demanding any longer. He had never been able to talk Thede into doing anything his father had set his will against doing.

"Well, what is your final answer?" he said, looking at Thede. "Yes, or no?"

"Yes, you're going to stay home and do the chores this winter. And no, by God, you're not leaving this house!"

"Is that your final answer?"

"It's the only answer I've ever made about this fool talk of yours. It's the first and the last. I've been telling you that ever since you started this fuss about studying bridge building. There's not another word to say. Now, shut up!"

Rosa, on the other side of the room smiling to herself, resumed her rocking in her squeaking chair.

Howard sat down at last, and almost immediately he tried to stand up again. He could make only one effort to

[107]

rise from the chair, because by that time he knew it would be useless for him to say another word to Thede.

He had been hearing his father talk like that all of his life, and it had always ended as it had this time. Always, his father had forced him to submit. He had never been able to shake off Thede's domination over him. He knew that it was in his blood, that tendency to yield to Thede's word. It was the Emerson blood, and the Frost blood. He did not, with that in him, have the courage to carry out his own will. But now something had to happen after this. He was certain of that. If he lost this time, it would be the last opportunity he would ever have. It would mean that forever after, as long as his father lived, he would have to submit to Thede's will without protest.

Howard sat before his father, wondering how he could ever overcome his tendency to be submissive.

Thede glanced once more at Howard, and then at Jean, and reached for his newspaper on the floor. He believed he had settled the matter for the last time, and he hoped he would have no more trouble with Howard after that.

Jean walked between Howard and their father.

"You're not going to let him make you stay here for the rest of your life, are you, Howard?" she asked calmly, looking directly at Thede. "You'd be working for him without pay as long as he lives, and then it would be too late for you to do anything for yourself." She turned and looked at her brother pleadingly. "Don't let him make you, Howard. Please, don't!"

"Now, you can shut up, young lady," Thede told her. "It's bad enough having a boy act like Howard, but I can handle women. You shut your mouth, and keep it shut. I don't care to hear more from you this evening."

Jean moved closer to her father.

"You may think you can make me shut up, but you can't. I'll take up for Howard as long as you treat him like this."

Thede got to his feet slowly and deliberately, glaring at Jean. He stood a step toward her, and then, before she knew what he was going to do, he had raised his hand and struck her on the face. She screamed with pain and fell at his feet.

"God damn you!" he shouted. "If there's anything I can't stand it's a blabbering bitch like you!"

He reached down and struck her again with his hand, harder than he had the first time. She covered her head with her arms and cried with pain.

Howard sprang toward his father, his fists clenched and white.

"I could knock you down for hurting her!"

He had barely finished shouting at his father when Thede struck him on the face with both fists. Thede stepped back, waiting to see what Howard would do.

"You won't hit me, no matter what I do," Thede said. "Now, go to bed. I don't wish to hear another word out of you this evening."

Howard stood solidly in front of his father, waiting as long as he could stand. His knees began to tremble and he had difficulty in keeping his balance. While Thede glared at him, his fists clenched ready to strike again if Howard advanced, he turned and walked from the room. He climbed the stairs heavily and went to bed.

Jean still lay on the floor beside the table, crying and shaking with sobs. Thede went to the door, shut it securely and came back beside her. There, he suddenly bent forward and struck her several times. Jean rolled over, crying out in pain, and tried to keep out of his reach.

"She needs some treatment like that," Rosa said approvingly, "and I'm glad to see her getting it at last. She needs smacking so hard she'll learn some sense. Somebody ought to do it, because she needs it now more than ever. Both Howard and her have wanted it all summer, and it's a good thing you started in on her when you did. It'll be too late once she's married and out of the house."

"Shut up, you!" Thede shouted at his wife. "I don't need any talk from you, either. I know how women ought to be handled, if they're going to be worth living with. I'd beat the blamed meanness out of you, if I'd do what I ought to. The trouble is, I've waited too long to start giving you what's due you. Now, shut up and stay shut up!"

Rosa smiled to herself, saying nothing more.

Thede bent over and hit Jean again, savagely and mercilessly. Her body trembled with pain when his hand struck her. She rolled as far away from him as she could, finally stopping when she could escape no farther than the corner.

Thede hesitated for several moments, as if deciding whether to hit her again or to leave her alone. After striking her once more, he reached down and jerked her off the floor to her feet. When she had gained her balance, he shoved her toward the door.

"Now, go to your room and stay there till I call you

out," he said. "And the next time you act like that I'll make it a whole lot worse for you. I know how to handle women, and I can still use a rope on either one of you if you cross me. Don't forget that. Now, get out!"

He shoved her again, so hard this time that she fell headlong on the floor before she could reach the wall for support. When she turned her head and saw Thede coming toward her, she jumped to her feet and ran up the stairs to her room as fast as she could.

CHAPTER XI

~~~~~~

WHEN JEAN AWOKE, SHE LAY STILL IN HER BED FOR A LONG time. It was later than she usually woke up in the morning, for the sun was already over the top of the maple tree beside her window. At first she had intended dressing and going downstairs for breakfast, but the longer she lay in bed, the less did she wish to go into the kitchen where Rosa was and be compelled to stay in the room with her for the rest of the morning.

Behind her closed eyes, the memory of what had taken place downstairs the evening before made her shudder and throw her arms around the pillow. The figure of her father, angrier than she had ever before seen him, advanced on her like the approach of a maddened wild animal. Before she was wide enough awake to know what she was doing, she had jumped screaming from the bed.

"Please don't!" she begged, running to the closet. "Papa, please don't hurt me!"

The sound of her own voice awakened her, and she could be calm again. The rays of the sun fell upon her as she stood at the closet door, and she knew that she had been dreaming.

"Dear God," she whispered, "please take me away and never let me have to come back as long as I live. I don't care what happens to me, but don't send me back here. I don't ever want to see this house again as long as I live — "

She opened her eyes then and looked out the window over the lake below Autmun Hill. The sun fell warm and comfortingly on her body. She ran to the window then and leaned far out, trying to get closer to the sun. While she stood there, she decided that she was not going downstairs and stay in the kitchen with Rosa. She would dress and go away somewhere. She would go some place where neither Rosa nor Thede could find her.

"When Frank and I are married, we'll never have to be with people who hate us," she said, dressing as quickly as she could. "There will be nobody to curse at us, and to hit us, and to tell us that we shan't be happy. All day long, and all night, year after year, we'll be happy. We'll never have to live with Mama and Papa. If I had to do that for the rest of my life, I'd rather die right now. I couldn't stand that."

As soon as she was ready, Jean tiptoed down the stairway and ran out the front door. Rosa was in the back of the house then, probably in the kitchen, and she did not hear her. When once she was out of the house, she knew that nothing could stop her. Neither Rosa nor Thede could call her back then, for even if they did see her, she was determined not to turn back or to stop.

She ran down the hillside toward the lake. The field was deep in grass, and she could not run fast because she had to watch for woodchuck holes. She knew that if she accidentally stepped into one of the holes while she was running, she would catch her foot in it and more than likely break her ankle. But she was already out of sight of the house, and she was no longer afraid of being seen and called back by her mother or father. When she reached the rocky shore of the lake, however, she did not stop. She turned to the right and went up the side of it, climbing over the huge boulders that had been washed free of earth by the waves. She was unable to run any longer, because the shore was piled high with drift logs and stones, but she could keep on going farther and farther away from Rosa and Autumn Hill.

There was a sandy beach a mile farther up the lake, and now that she had had time to think of some place where she might go, she decided to go there and to lie on the sand in the warm sun. No one would see her there, because the beach was hidden from the road and the motorboats and canoes of fishermen and hunters passed along the main channel a quarter of a mile in the distance. She knew she could stay there as long as she wished and never be discovered. Thede and Rosa, even if they attempted to find her, would never come that far in search of her.

As she climbed over the round smooth boulders, which had been eroded and polished by the high waves of the spring storms, she wondered about Howard again. No matter how happy she was when she was with Frank, she had never been able to banish from mind the certainty that Howard would always be unhappy as long as he had to stay at Autumn Hill.

She wondered what would happen if she ran away from

home now and never went back. It was something she had never thought of doing before, and she wondered if she would be courageous enough to do such a thing. The thought had been frightening at first, but the longer she thought about it, the greater was her inclination to leave home. If she did that, she reasoned to herself, her brother might have the courage to follow her example and go away, too. It might even be the only thing she could ever do for him during their father's lifetime — something that would free him from the domination of Thede and Rosa and give him the opportunity to live his life the way he wanted to live it. It seemed certain to her then that if he stayed at Autumn Hill for the next twenty or thirty years, in the end he would become as unreasonable and prejudiced as their father was.

Walking faster, she was almost at the sandy shore before she realized it. There was a short stretch of marsh along the shore, and when she reached it, she stopped and took off her shoes and stockings so she would not get them wet. The ground was not so wet that she could not have crossed the marsh while wearing her slippers, but after she had reached the other side she was glad she had removed them. The warm boulders under her bare feet felt just as good as the sun did on her face. She ran a short distance, and then she was on the beach.

Tossing her slippers and stockings aside, Jean fell face downward on the warm clean sand and lay there for a long time without moving. The sun beat down upon her neck and arms, sending streams of warmth through her body. It was so pleasant there on the sand, with the sun so warm and the breeze from the lake so clean and cool, that Jean could not believe that she was actually there instead of being in the house with her mother and father. She dug her hands into the sand, burying them and uncovering them over and over again.

When she stopped, her eyes were blinded and everything was a swimming blackness. She dropped her head on the sand, closing her eyes and waiting for the blackness to go away.

"We can't help ourselves any more," she said, as though she were talking to someone beside her. "I've tried and Howard has tried. But it's no use. We can't do anything that they have set themselves against. This is the only chance we have left."

She thought she had been asleep for a long time when she suddenly sat up and looked around her. The sand-prints on her arms were deep and sharp. She jumped to her feet and looked at the sun.

"If there were only some other way to help Howard," she said. "Any way — except running away — because I'd be running away from Frank, too."

She walked to the boulders behind her and climbed over them. On the other side, where the forest came down to the shore, there was a wall of blackberry bushes that grew between the trees and the rocks. She climbed over and sat down on a boulder beside the bushes. The blackberries were ripe, and she had to be careful not to shake the bushes, lest they should all fall off before she could get them. She gathered as many as she thought she could eat and carried them back to the beach in the apron of her skirt. There she sat down on the sand and ate them.

The sun shone warmer and warmer, but she knew that within another two hours it would begin to go down behind the hills across the lake and that it would then become cool again. She wished the sun would not go down. It was so pleasant, and so far away from Autumn Hill, that she could almost forget that there was a house there with Rosa and Thede in it. When she closed her eyes, Autumn Hill seemed to be beyond all existence.

Speaking softly to herself, she said, "I don't know what to do about Howard. He's my brother, and I want to help him. Nobody else in the whole world will — or can help him. But what's to happen to me? Shouldn't I think of myself — a little bit? I may never have another chance to be happy as long as I live. If I give up Frank in order to try to help Howard — maybe it wouldn't do either one of us much good in the end. And then it would be too late. Frank might find somebody else — but I never would! I could never love anybody else — Frank is the only one!"

She opened her eyes and looked around her in the bright sunlight. Her whole body began to tremble.

"Dear God, don't let me go away . . . even to help Howard. Keep me with Frank as long as I live . . . no matter what happens to Howard. He's got to take care of himself now. Mama was right . . . I do like Howard too much . . . much too much. I've got to quit thinking about him. Please, God, let me stop thinking about him! If I lose Frank now, I'll never be able to love anybody else — except Howard! I know it! It's true! Mama knows how true it is — and I do, too, now. . . . But, Dear God, please help Howard — I can't, after this. It's too late now. . . ."

Not bothering to take off her dress, Jean ran out into the water and fell face downward upon the waves. At first she felt as though she wished to stay there forever and never leave the comfort of the cool lake, but gradually the tingling cold of the water made her body shiver convulsively, and presently she got to her feet and waded back to shore. When her feet touched the warm sand of the beach, the sun was sinking behind the forest.

She was ready then to go back home to Autumn Hill.

CHAPTER XII

For nearly an hour Rosa had been sitting on the bole of a storm-blown maple two hundred yards off the back road. When she had first got there, she had broken a dead limb into two short pieces and stuck them into the ground. That was for her one means of reckoning time; the other way, far less accurate, was to try to remember how long she had been there. As the sun moved, the shadow cast by the trees moved, and when the shadow reached the second stick, Rosa knew that she had been waiting for Leland Stokes much longer than she wished to wait.

Several large gray squirrels had been barking overhead all the time she had been there, and as long as she remained still, they did not resent her presence. They came running down the trees to the ground to sit and look at her, but only to turn suddenly after a few moments and run away again.

"Get away!" she said irritably.

The squirrels ran, but they went only as far away as the first limbs of the trees. They sat there, scolding and barking for having been driven off.

Leland had promised to meet Rosa again on the tote

road, which was only a mile from Autumn Hill, at three o'clock that afternoon. Usually he was on time, but Rosa had always got to the meeting place first. Sometimes she would go there an hour before the time that had been set, and would wait impatiently for him to come. Today she had waited an hour, and Leland was half an hour late. Rosa knew he would come, though; he had never failed to meet her and he would not dare to stay away now.

The dress she had put on just before leaving home was the one she had ordered for Jean and which Jean had handed over to her when she discovered how large it was. She had been saving it all that time, waiting for the first cool day of fall before wearing it, and now that she had put it on for the first time, she felt that she was better dressed than she had been in several years. The youthful cut of the dress, with its low neck and long sleeves, gave her a feeling of being young again.

"Get away!" she said sharply to the squirrels.

Rosa spoke as snappishly as she felt at the moment. She was cross because Leland had not come an hour ahead of time, as she did, and she was angry because she knew he would like to leave sooner than she did. She wished each time to stay there in the woods until dark, but Leland always had some excuse to offer for being in a hurry to get back to the village. Either he would say he had to see a man who wanted a calf or hog butchered, or else he would say there was a task at his house that had to be done before evening. Anyway, those were the two most frequently used excuses he made when she insisted on his telling her why he must leave. Rosa thought that four hours was not too long to stay in the woods with Leland; he, however, always acted as though he wished to leave after they had been together for only half an hour or less. Generally she was able to make him stay with her until sunset, but she was continually afraid that he would jump up at any minute and plead that he had to go home at once.

"Get away from here!" Rosa said peevishly. "Leave me alone!" The squirrels raced back up the tree and watched her attentively.

This time, in an effort to improve her appearance and make herself more attractive to Leland Stokes, Rosa had used a white face powder. It was spread thickly over the dark skin of her face, but she had neglected to apply it to the slightly wrinkled and darkly tanned skin of her neck. On her cheeks she had used rouge. The rouge was the shade of a sun-ripened tomato, and against her powdered white face the contrast was startling. The shade of red that she had colored her lips was even more brilliant than her rouged cheeks, and against her chalky white face it gave her the appearance of a cheaply and carelessly made china doll.

She rubbed the end of a finger over her lips. Without a mirror she could not see what she was doing, but she could feel the outline of her mouth, and she tried to spread the lipstick evenly. Then she wiped the red paste from her finger on the hem of her stockings. It was time for Leland to come, for the shadow had moved all the way from one stick to the other. More than an hour had already passed, and she knew he should be coming at almost any minute. She listened for the sound of his automobile down the road, but the big gray squirrels were barking so loudly she could not hear anything else.

"Shut up!" she yelled at them.

The squirrels stopped at the first sound of her voice, and remained still on the limbs overhead. They looked down at her with their big round eyes watching her as though she were some strange animal that they had never before encountered.

"Shut up! You fools, you!" she said.

During the next minute's silence she heard an automobile coming down the back road from the direction of the village. She knew it was Leland by the sound of the motor's exhaust, and she could judge from it that he was only a short distance away. It would take him two or three minutes to reach the tote road, turn into it, and come to where she was.

She got up and smoothed her dress and adjusted her stockings. She wet her lips with her tongue.

The squirrels ran off out of sight when Leland drove his car up the tote road and stopped.

"Well," Rosa said, walking over to the automobile.

"Can't stay long this time," Leland said at once, getting out and shutting the door. "Have to get back and —"

"How do you like my new dress, Leland?"

"Is that it?" he said, stepping back and looking at her. "It's not so bad, I guess."

"This is the first time I've worn it. Been keeping it all summer to wear down here sometime."

Leland went off into the woods. Rosa followed him. He walked until they were out of sight of the automobile.

"Guess this will be a good place," he said, sitting down on the pine needles.

Rosa remained standing in front of him.

"Well, aren't you going to kiss me some?"

"Don't know but what I shall," he said. "Come here."

She sat down beside him. He turned and looked at her face. She waited for him to kiss her, while he continued to stare at her mouth.

"What's that you've got on you?" he asked, still staring at her crimson lips.

"Oh, just something."

"Don't care to have it all over me."

Rosa bent over and wiped some of it on the hem of her petticoat.

Leland took off his coat and spread it on the leaves beside them. While she waited for him to kiss her, he leaned back on his elbows.

"Have got to hurry back home," Leland said.

"No, you haven't, Leland."

"Have got to."

"What for?"

"Can't lose the time."

"Don't talk like that again today, Leland. Stay a long while now. The last time you stayed only about half an hour. There is no sense in you saying every time to hurry up so you can go back to the village. When you get there, you don't do anything but sit in the barbershop and talk. Stay here with me, Leland."

Leland stretched out on his back and put his hands under his head. He looked up at the trees for a long time. While he was not looking at her, Rosa moved closer to him and laid her hand on his leg. They were both still for several minutes, neither speaking.

"Come on, Leland," Rosa said.

"What's the hurry?"

"Leland, come on."

"What do you wish?"

"Come on, Leland."

"Will kiss you in a minute."

"A minute is a long time to wait. I've been waiting ever since you got here, but you haven't done it yet."

"Would like to rest a minute or two," he said, closing his eyes. "Didn't have much time to rest before I left home. Was working all morning."

"Leland, hurry up!"

"What's Jean doing now?" he asked, slowly turning toward her.

"Don't know what she's doing," Rosa said.

"Is she at home? Guess she is getting ready to marry Gervais, isn't she? Wish she wouldn't marry him. If I had my way about it, I wouldn't let her marry yet for a while. Maybe somebody else will wish to marry her. A man with some property and money would be better for her. It looks like she don't care for older men, though. A man my age with property would treat her as good as Frank Gervais will. Maybe I'd treat her a lot better. Could buy for her little things with money."

Rosa leaned closer to him.

"Why don't you ask her if she wouldn't rather marry somebody else? Say a man like me, for instance. She ought to wait and marry somebody who has got enough money and property so she won't have to work all the time. She will have to work pretty hard for Gervais. He hasn't got anything, not even a farm and buildings paid for. You ought to say something to her about it. Could buy for her little things with money."

"It's none of your business about her," Rosa said. "You quit thinking about her like that."

Leland looked off into the woods for a moment before turning to look at Rosa. Her body seemed to spread wider than ever on the ground. He looked at her steadily, as though he wondered why he was there with her. He was always eager to meet her, but once they were together he could not understand why they met so often.

"Come on, Leland," Rosa said impatiently. "Hurry up!"

The sun was sinking lower and lower, and it was getting late in the afternoon.

"Leland!"

"Guess Jean wouldn't turn down a man like me, if she knew me better," he said. "It wouldn't do any harm for you to say something to her about it, before it's too late. There's no sense in her marrying Gervais, if she would take to another man a little later on, somebody like me who would treat her good. If she married Gervais first, it would sort of ruin her for me. I'd like to be the first to upset her. Have got some money and a little property. Would buy her what she needs. Could buy for her little things with money."

Rosa jerked at Leland, pulling his arm and throwing herself against him.

"Leland!" she said, angered. "Hurry up!"

"You still waiting for me to kiss you?" he said. "Well, all right."

Rosa bent over him eagerly and placed her lips against his. She began kissing him the moment their lips touched. Her mouth felt to Leland as if it were becoming larger and larger each second. With a sudden tightening in his throat he pushed her away. Rosa would not release him, though; she held him closer, finally pulling him over against her. Slowly he felt himself being drawn with her, and after that he could not get out of her embrace.

"Now," she said hoarsely. "Now, Leland!"

"Will you speak to Jean about me being her man?"

"No!" she said. "You quit thinking that!"

After all these months, Leland still hoped to be able to persuade Rosa to send Jean to meet him in the woods. Without constant hope and anticipation, he knew he would not have forced himself to endure Rosa's company as long as he had. Each time he met Rosa he hoped she would relent and promise to send Jean the next time. There were times, especially when Rosa was afraid Leland would fail to come back the next time, when she led him to believe that she would send Jean. On other occasions she tried to interest him so much that he would not want to think of anyone else.

"Time's gone by pretty fast," Leland said presently. "You'll have to hurry if you're going to keep your promise."

"What promise, Leland?" she asked.

"What you said once about sending Jean."

"That wasn't a promise — I said maybe I would sometime."

"But she's getting married. Time's growing short."

"And I'm glad of it," Rosa said angrily. "Maybe after that you'll quit talking about her so much and think about me some."

"I'd hate to have to hold it against you that you lied about it and never meant to do what you promised."

"I told you it wasn't a promise."

"Well, if it wasn't, it was so close to it that it meant the same thing. I don't like to be fooled. I don't like it one bit."

"Now, Leland," Rosa said, pleadingly. "Please, Leland."

He suddenly pushed her away from him.

"No, Leland!" she said desperately, clutching him tightly. "Stay with me, Leland!"

He was ready to leave and he wanted to get away from her as quickly as possible. He had been there for half an hour and everything after that moment was disagreeable. He had no desire for her.

Once more he tried to get to his feet, and again Rosa clung tightly to him.

"I can be good to you, Leland. You know I can. You used to tell me how good I was to you. Don't you remember, Leland? I don't want you to be thinking about anybody else. You don't have to, if you'll let me keep on being good to you. You won't regret it."

"Times change," he said shortly. "Don't want to let myself be foolish."

"Let me tell you something, Leland. If you'll keep on coming to meet me, there'll be a time when you'll be glad you did. I'm going to inherit a good share of all that money when he dies, and I'll be willing to treat you right about it. There won't be anything to keep us from getting married then, either. Now, can you see what there is in store for you?"

"Haven't joined up legally with any woman yet, and don't know that I ever shall wish to."

"We won't have to get married, after he's dead and I've inherited the money. But I'll share it with you, Leland."

"Don't observe any signs of his getting ready to die for a long time to come yet. He looks mighty hale and hearty to me every time I chance upon him. He might even outlive me. Sure would feel like a fool then."

Rosa was breathing deeply beside him. He glanced at her for a moment and then turned his head away. He hoped he would never see her again as she looked then, but he knew he would continue to meet her as long as she had any use for him. Nothing that he could say or do would cause her power over him to go away. He would come the next time, and the next and the next. He would come as long as there was any hope of Rosa sending Jean in her stead.

After another five minutes, Leland thought he would surely grasp her neck in his hands and squeeze the life out of her if she did not stop and let him alone. She had no control over herself, and no regard for the way she handled him. She was forcing him by her strength to stay with her. He did not know how he was going to keep from killing her if she did not soon stop.

When he knew he had reached the limit of his endurance, and when he felt himself on the verge of using violence to stop her treatment of him, she suddenly pushed him to one side and grabbed his hand. He felt his hand being held against her with both of hers, but he was unable to feel anything but complete relief after being held to her for such a length of time. When he had turned and looked at her then, he was thankful that she had at last finished with him. She lay panting and sweating, her face a contorted smear of red paint. Beads of perspiration had burst through her cheeks, making the rouge trickle in thin streams like blood to her throat. He wished momentarily that he had allowed himself to choke her when he had first tried to. Then he would never have had to meet her again and live through other hours of agony. However, as long as there was hope of someday having Jean take Rosa's place, he knew he would keep on coming there.

He got up slowly and walked back to the tote road where he had left his car. He did not know how long he had been forced to remain with Rosa this time, but it seemed like many hours to him then.

While he was starting the motor, Rosa came running through the brush, her stockings falling around her ankles, her hair flying in all directions, and her dress held in folds around her thick thighs. She came and caught the door so he could not close it and leave. She did not say anything then, and she did not expect him to speak. She merely stood there and prevented him from leaving. He turned his head to escape the sight of her. He hated Rosa more than he ever had before.

"Next Tuesday," she said after a while. "Will meet you here next Tuesday at three o'clock."

"Don't know if I can spare the time, come next Tuesday," he said slowly. "Have considerable affairs to attend."

Rosa gazed at him severely, saying nothing.

"That's right," he said with an emphatic nod of his head. "Going to be somewhat busy, attending important affairs."

She came a little closer. "Would you be satisfied, just once? Would you stop talking about it after that, Leland?"

His face brightened. "What do you mean, Rosa?"

"Just what I said."

"I never was one to go back on my word, if I made a honest promise, Rosa. I wouldn't want to be forced to say something against my will, though. That's why a lot of times a promise can do more harm than good, all things considered. Now, if you'd just ask me face-to-face if I want to do what's right —"

"Leland, if I should be busy in the house and can't get here myself, I'll send Jean next Tuesday."

He stared at her momentarily. "You will?" he said in a low tone. "You'll send her instead?"

Rosa nodded.

"Well," he said, smiling quickly, "that'll be all right with me, Rosa. You do that. It'll be just fine and dandy."

Rosa turned and walked stiffly away from him, going in the direction of the path that would take her back to Autumn Hill. He waited until she had gone several yards, and then he slammed the door of the car and quickly started the engine. He turned the car around and drove toward the road without looking at Rosa again.

CHAPTER XIII

THE MEN IN ROBINSON'S STORE HAD BEEN WAITING HALF an hour or longer for a new topic of conversation to arise. Most of them had been sitting there on counters and in chairs since dinner and, as usual, there was very little said until someone thought of a subject to talk about that would be of interest to them all. The store was not so full as it generally was at that time of day, because a large number of townsmen were away from home that week attending the agricultural fair and harness racing in North Somerset.

Ben had seen Thede Emerson drive into the village in his old car ten or fifteen minutes before, and he knew that it would not be long until he came into the store. Thede had not, for all of twenty years, put his foot on the inside of Frost's store. Webster Frost once had charged him ten cents for a nickel package of salt and, although Thede had paid the overcharge without a single word of protest or comment, he never went back there again after that. Robinson's was the only other store in the village, and the men who had seen him drive into the street half an hour earlier knew that Thede would come there before going back home. There was no other place for him to go, except to the post office, to the clothespin mill, or to the barbershop; and only the post office was open then. If he should go there, he would certainly not stay more than a minute or two in the company of Hormidas Doucette.

One of the men got up and went to the door, looking up and down the street to see where Thede was. He came back presently saying that Thede was then on his way to the store.

"Don't guess Thede offered to buy Hormidas a cigar," Arthur White said. "Sometimes I should just like to get those two together somewhere and make them talk — or fight. What Thede Emerson would say would be worth writing down to keep. Guess Hormidas would speak up for himself, though, in the best of company. He's not afraid of any man's presence, and Thede knows it. Hormidas is a fine fellow in many ways. I've always taken a liking to Hormidas. He's been a good friend of mine for a long time."

"Must have French blood somewhere in your family, Arthur," Ben said. "Whenever I hear a townsman sticking up for the French, I always say he would make a blamed good Canuck himself."

Everybody laughed then, but before anyone could reply, Thede walked through the door. He had left the post office and had walked across the street with his newspaper under his arm. He laid it aside when he came in, putting it where he would be certain to see it when he got ready to leave for home.

"Blamed if it's not Thede Emerson," Ben said. "We've

just been talking about you, indirectly, Thede. Maybe you can tell us something. You look like you're cheerful all over after having a nice long chat with Hormidas over there in the post office."

Thede paid no attention to what was being said, but when he heard Doucette's name mentioned, he looked sharply at all the men. He turned finally, glaring at Ben Robinson.

"What's that about Doucette?" he said.

"Was just remarking how chummy you were with Hormidas," Ben said. "It used to be that you wouldn't even go near the post office. Nowadays, the first thing you do when you come to the village is to walk right in, stay a long time, and come out smiling all over. What's happened to you, Thede? Have you taken a liking to Hormidas?"

Everybody laughed when Ben said that. Ben sat down in his buggy-backed chair and waited for Thede to reply.

"Guess there's funnier things than that to laugh about," Thede said. "I've got now, and have always had, just about as much use for that Doucette as I have for a brown bear in my cultivated raspberries, tramping down the bushes. I'm letting my girl marry a Frenchman, but I'll be blamed if that isn't as far as I'll go. Me and Frenchmen don't hitch well together, that's all."

"Thede's got a natural-grown grudge against all foreign fellows," Lincoln said. "I've never heard Thede Emerson say a good word for a foreigner yet, and I don't aim to hear one before I die, either."

"And you never will," Thede said. "Not when I'm in my right mind, you won't."

"That reminds me of something, Thede," Ben said. "The invitation you passed around for the wedding still holds good, doesn't it?"

"Never intend to mean it more than I do this minute. Wish to see everybody there."

"Well, I'm glad to hear you say that, Thede, because I had my wife wash out my new undershirt and fancy drawers last evening, preparatory to going to the wedding next week at Autumn Hill."

"Ben's lying," somebody beyond his hearing said to the men nearest him. "Ben's wife didn't wash them out for him. Flora Randolph washes out Ben's shirts and drawers. He's just scared to mention her name — that's why he said his wife did it. Ben's wife hasn't turned her hand over for him in fourteen-fifteen years."

"I don't go back on what I say," Thede answered. "Still looking for every man and woman in the town of Clearwater out at Autumn Hill. And come early, because there's nine barrels of last-crop cider waiting to be drunk."

"Haven't changed your mind about letting Jean marry Frank Gervais, have you? Shouldn't like to go all the distance out there to Autumn Hill under the impression that I was going to witness Thede Emerson's daughter marry a Frenchman, and then get there to find that you'd changed your mind about it and was making her marry a Frost or a Walton instead."

"Jean's marrying Gervais," Thede said, "and damn the man who says a word against it. I've made my plans for that, and I won't change them now. I shouldn't like to see her starve to death this winter, if she didn't freeze first,

[134]

marrying a Robinson or Walton, or any of the rest of them."

"Can't take your insult, Thede, because there's only one male Robinson left in Clearwater Town, and my wife wouldn't grant me leave to marry a young girl brought up under the Emerson roof. She wouldn't trust me to do that."

Everybody laughed at Ben Robinson's joke. Even Thede smiled a little at what he had said.

"It's nobody's fault but your own, that there's no more Robinsons except you left," George Walton said. "Though there's the chance that if you did have some children, they probably wouldn't have your name, anyway."

"There's a considerable difference between wanting them, George, and the getting of them. Guess us Robinsons are just plain petered out. Won't no children come. I've tried like a man, but my wife don't ever show signs of breeding. The Waltons and the Frosts petered out long ago, and now the rest of us are coming to the same pass. Won't none of our names be left here in Clearwater after the present ones have died off. That is, except on the headstones in the cemetery."

"Thede ought to try to persuade Frank Gervais to change his name to Emerson," Lincoln said. "If that was done, then there'd be Emersons here long afterward, maybe always."

"I've got a son of my own to maintain the Emerson name and keep it alive," Thede told them. "That's something I don't have to worry about. Howard will be continuing where I leave off. Autumn Hill and the Emersons shall be here in Clearwater Town as long as the country lasts, maybe even after that. Not even those French and Portuguese, with all their big gristle and festivous women, will be able to crowd the Emersons out of the town. I couldn't repose peacefully in my grave, under the snow of winter or the green sod of summer, if there wasn't an Emerson left living to light a lamp and put it in the window at nightfall to boast the family pride."

"That depends on what girl he marries with the aim of having children by," George said, glancing around the store. "The boy can't continue the name of Emerson unless he marries a girl who can bear children. He'll have to go to the French or the Scandinavians for that, too. Granted that he's not petered out himself."

"But I thought Howard was going up to Boston to stay in a college," Ben said. "Didn't he go the first of the week, when the time came?"

"Howard is staying at home to work at Autumn Hill," Thede said. "He didn't go up to Boston, because I told him to stay at home where he belongs."

Lincoln wished to say something, but he knew by the way that Thede had spoken, and by the way he looked now, that it would be useless to question Thede further about Howard. He knew that Howard had not given up without putting up a fight.

After a while Ben started talking again.

"You can swear at the Frenchmen and Scandinavians all you care to, but they spend a lot of money in the stores. If I had to depend for a living on the trade that comes from the other townsmen, I'd have to get into some other line of business. If I continued to run a store and had to depend on all my trade coming from our kind of townsmen, I could do that mostly sitting at home and opening up the store only two-three days a week."

"They're spending money, all right," Thede said, "but they're taking it out of our own pockets to spend for themselves. There's only so much money to be had, and when the foreigners get through taking what they wish, there's never much left over for the rest of us."

"A man with two hundred thousand dollars in the bank hasn't any right to talk like that," somebody said. "You've got your share, and more besides. Blamed if I won't say that you've got my share too, because I haven't got it. Money ought to be spread out. Some of these days men like you will have to put up a fight to keep it. Every human ought to have enough food to provide for a comfortable belly. There are days when me and my family don't eat fully."

"I worked for what I got," Thede replied sharply. "Didn't sit loafing all the time around Ben Robinson's store and begrudging the money to those true townsmen who had sweated and earned what they had."

Nothing was said for several moments.

"Haven't got a thing in the world against the foreigners as customers," Ben said after a while. "I'd just as soon sell a sack of flour to Alarak Henata as I would to John Childs, and a little more so, to tell the whole truth, because Alarak pays cash for what he buys and John Childs makes the bill run awhile, six-seven months sometimes."

Lincoln stretched out his feet, clearing his throat. Thede turned around so he could hear what Lincoln had to say.

"Still swearing at the foreigners, are you?" Lincoln

began. "Well, when we're dead and done and in the ground, this town will be a blamed better sight off than it is now. The young folks who're coming along now are growing up with the French and Swedes, and they're liking them. Thede's daughter is marrying one of them next week, and others are doing it more and more all the time in every part of the state. Nissen, Doucette, Hedenstjerna, Nordenskjold, and all such men coming down here was the best thing that ever happened to us. If they hadn't come when they did — well, we would have had to turn the place over to the federal government to keep up for the wild animals."

"Or the rats," George Walton said. "If the federal government wouldn't have the town, the rats would. That reminds me of something I saw. I saw the biggest drove of rats the day before yesterday I ever hope to see again in all my life. I was sitting home, when my wife called me and said, 'George, for the love of God, come look at this sight!' I said, 'What is it?' She said, 'The rats, George! God have pity on us!' Well, I ran to the window and looked out across the field, and I'll be blamed if there wasn't a drove of them that made the ground hidden from sight for a space as big as a two-acre garden. Those rats were almost as large as little black dogs, and fatter, if you ask me, and they were moving over the field like they knew where they came from and where they were going. Guess they were vacating the cannery, now that the corn and bean season is over, and were moving up the hillside to somebody's house and barn. I hope they like it where they went and don't change their minds and come back to my buildings."

"Can put up with the rats and woodchucks," Thede said, "and summer-people, too. But I'll be blamed if all of them put together are as pesty as the foreigners in the State of Maine."

"That reminds me of another thing," George said. "My wife told me to bring her a can of peaches. How much are your peaches bringing today, Ben?"

"The regular price has always been thirty cents for a large-sized can."

"Thirty cents?" George said. "Now, how much do you sell them to the summer-people for?"

"Thirty cents."

George reached into his pocket and drew out a leather wallet. He untied the drawstrings and took out two dimes and a nickel and laid the coins on the counter.

"I'll be taking a can of the large size at the irregular price," he said.

Ben looked at the money several moments before picking it up and dropping the coins into the cash box.

"You can't talk George into paying more for the peaches than the can is worth," Lincoln said. "He will pay the right price, but he won't pay you the summer-people's price, Ben. George will let you know he was born and raised and lived all his life in the village here."

Ben wrapped the can of peaches in a piece of paper and laid it on the counter beside George. George felt so good over the fact that he thought he had saved a nickel that he did not notice that the can Ben gave him was the smaller size.

"Thanks," George said, putting his wallet back into

his pocket. "Don't ever let me forget to pay you the right price for my purchases, Ben. If I was to accidently pay you like I was a summer visitor, and was to find out about it later, I should never be able to hold my head up straight again."

"Nobody mistakes you for a summer visitor," Lincoln said. "Summer-people don't come around asking for the price of things, such as peaches. They buy them first and then they ask what the worth is. That's the way you can tell a summer visitor anywhere in the state."

Two or three of the men got up and left the store. It was close to five o'clock then, and Thede glanced at his watch several times trying to make up his mind whether he wished to go home just then or to wait another quarter hour.

Ben had got up to wait on a customer who asked for a loaf of baker's bread, and he came back to his buggy-backed chair and sat down beside Thede.

"How's your family getting along now, Thede?" he asked. "Now that you are getting your girl married, and have got the boy settled down, what about the rest of the house? I guess, though, that if you can handle a young girl and boy, you can take care of your wife's doings, can't you?"

Thede looked sharply at Ben, but he was surprised not to find himself angry with him. Some of the other men waited to hear what kind of an answer Thede could make to that question. There had been several new rumors around the town and in the village recently. Most everyone in the store wished to hear what Thede had to say now.

"Expect I shall be losing my wife one of these days," Thede said, matter-of-factly.

"Your wife?" Ben said. "Didn't know you ever had much more than a housekeeper out there for the past twenty years, Thede. That is, going by what I've heard about her off and on all this time."

"Well, Rosa is a lot younger than I am. I'm an old man now, Ben. I'm leaning toward seventy. Rosa is barely forty now. That makes a difference. She's got ideas in her head, too. No sense trying to keep a woman held down when she wishes to do something else. She'll keep the house raised full of dust, day and night, if she can't have her own way."

"You ought to be able to please her, Thede. She's not so much that a man like you can't take care of her."

"Guess I could give her money, if that's what you're speaking of, but it's not always money she wishes. She's got her head set for a younger man. I don't blame her much, either. Guess if I was forty and she was sixty-seventy, I would be after doing likewise."

"Give her a divorce, then," Ben said. "That will take her off your hands and care for all time. A lot of women nowadays are never satisfied till they've had one or two divorces."

"Rosa doesn't wish a divorce, and I don't care to give her one, either. She just would like to be free to come and go when she feels like it, and as long as she does her household work like it should be done, and cooks my meals and keeps things clean about the place, I'm satisfied. That makes both of us satisfied as long as things go along like they are now. She doesn't care to lose her share of my estate by divorcing me, and I don't blame her there, either. But I'm losing her in other ways to a younger man. There's no getting around that."

"If she was my wife, I would let her go and stay gone. And I'd be blamed if I'd let her come back after she'd had her fun somewhere else, either. There's no female anywhere worth taking back once she's been mixed up somewhere else. That's what I'd do, Thede. I should let her go and stay gone."

None of the other men was inclined to talk about Rosa in Thede's presence. They listened, however, to every word that was said.

"It's a funny thing, us two talking like this," Ben said. "All us old men sitting around here talking about things like that strikes me pretty hard. Guess it happens every year about this time, though. It's the fall and early winter coming on again. All the summer-people have left and now we haven't got anything to talk about except our troubles. I can remember hearing such things going on for the past twenty-thirty years, and it's always been about this same time of year, too. It's the fall and early winter coming on again. Seems like now is the time when the old die off, the middle-aged go crazy, and the young commit suicide. Now is the season of the year when the farms are abandoned and the married have their divorces.

"Guess this is the hind tit of the Union, down here where we are, after all. Don't guess such things happen anywhere else in the whole world now, except down-Maine. But it wasn't always so in the past, and I'd have been the first to damn any man who claimed it was. It must be the kind of people we've grown to be that makes it happen like it does now. Can't see any other reason for solid men like me and you, Lincoln and George, and all the rest of us true townsmen petering out and just sitting back to give leave to things happening when, how, and where they have a will to. It's the early autumn and hard winter coming on that brings it about. Looks like all such things come about at a season of the year, and the time to be dreaded is coming over us again. Dwelling houses without lighted windows at nightfall are getting to be as common a sight as pesky milkweed pods shedding floss in August."

CHAPTER XIV

~~~~~~

NOTHING WAS SAID FOR A WHILE, AND AFTER SEVERAL MINutes Thede noisily cleared his throat.

"Can't deny the truth of some of what you say," Thede remarked. "We've got too many abandoned farms in the town for our good. You can't collect taxes from people who you can't see with your eyes or hear tell of by word of mouth. There's nothing that makes me sadder than the sight of so many dark houses."

"It's that creeping forest," Ben said. "That's what scares folks away from the back-road farms and makes them go to the cities. That forest is going to creep over all of us, houses and people alike, before it quits — and it never quits. It's been creeping back over the cleared fields and croplands ever since I can remember, and I'm getting to be an old man. As long as I've been here to watch it, no matter how early in the forenoon a man gets up to whack at it, the blamed trees spring right back through the earth to stare us in the face. It won't be much longer till there'll be few like us to keep the forest out of the dooryards and to set lighted lamps in the windows at nightfall."

"Autumn Hill will be here for a long time to come,"

Thede asserted determinedly. "I've taken steps to see to that. I'm leaving a son behind to drive back the forest. And he'll light the lamp at nightfall and set it on the window sill, just like I've always done. Autumn Hill is going to be here. I've made up my mind to that."

"The hill will always be there, Thede, because the snow and rain aren't capable of wearing the rock away, but I shouldn't be any too certain about the farm and buildings. There used to be dozens of farms just as fine as Autumn Hill ever was, but you can't locate them in the new forest now. The farms were abandoned and left to grow up in juniper and trees. The people just weren't here any longer to live there. You know what is happening to the townsmen as well as I do, Thede."

"But I've got a son to live at Autumn Hill and keep it in repair and fight back the new forest when I'm dead," Thede protested. "He'll keep it in repair and beat the forest back when I'm dead and gone. A new coat of white-lead paint every two-three years, and a new steel roof on the house inside nine-ten years, will preserve it for a long time yet to come. I couldn't die easy and lie peacefully in the ground if I thought Autumn Hill would stay to be abandoned and grown up in white birches. I'd have to get up out of my coffin and go out and fight back the brush. I couldn't stand such a sight as that."

"Wouldn't be so sure about the farm and buildings lasting much longer than you are alive," Ben shook his head. "Autumn Hill isn't a bit different from what the other fine farms in Clearwater and the nearby towns used to be. There was a time when there were dozens of them, maybe hundreds, thirty-forty-fifty years ago. You can remember that time as well as I do, Thede. God Himself can't keep back the forest off the hayfields and the juniper off the pastures — unless He keeps on sending the French and Scandinavians and Russians to take our places."

"That can't happen to Autumn Hill, Ben. My head is set against it. I've got a male child to live there when I'm dead and gone, and I guess Rosa will be here awhile after I'm gone, too. There'll always be Emersons living at Autumn Hill. It's the way I wish things to be. Wouldn't like to have that blamed new forest creep over my farm and buildings."

"The trouble with you, Thede, is that you can't believe what anybody tells you for a fact. If you could believe what I say, then you'd know how likely it is to happen to Autumn Hill. Autumn Hill and the Emersons are no different from the Edwardses and the Hopkinses who can't be found at their homesteads now."

Thede had already begun to suspect that Ben Robinson knew what he was talking about. He tried not to pay any attention to Ben's prophecies, but he could not banish from his mind the thoughts they provoked. This was the one thing all his life he had tried to keep from thinking about with any seriousness. It was now almost impossible for him to believe the truth, even though he knew that the chances were that Ben was right. It was not a matter of personal opinion; it was the inevitable he tried to ignore. He feared that it was as certain as the creep of the forest, and every bit as inescapable. Thede did not know how to get around that. God seemed to be the moving force in such things, and he had never been able to understand God. That was why he was not a church member and why he never attended religious services. He could not understand some things, and he had always tried to evade what he was incapable of comprehending. Now though, when he was nearing the end of his life, he hoped that if God could direct the destiny of the world, He would be able to take care of Autumn Hill.

"You look like you don't believe a word of what I'm telling you," Ben said. "You're a man of enough sense to have seen just what I'm talking about. Everybody with sense knows such things, Thede. It took me almost fifteen years to find out the truth, and I nearly missed knowing about it then."

"Tell me how it could happen — how Autumn Hill could be left to be covered with juniper and forest."

Ben laughed and looked out the front of the store. Something he had thought of had made him unable to keep from laughing, even though Thede was so serious about the matter. Thede looked at him scornfully.

"Are you laughing at me?" he demanded, glaring at Ben. "What's so funny to laugh at?"

"Couldn't help laughing, Thede. Just happened to think that here we are, you and me, talking about farms and buildings being abandoned and rotting and growing up in white birches, and out there in the street is that crowd of young Canuck boys talking about doing things. That's what's so funny. Those Bedard boys, and the young Dube, and the Fortiners, are talking about making things and growing things, and here we are, me and you, old and petered out, sitting here and talking about things rotting. It helps to prove what I've been telling you, anyway."

Thede turned and looked for a moment at the group of young men standing in the street. They were French, he could see that at a glance, and they were probably discussing their jobs in the mills and talking over what they indended doing the following year. Thede knew, just as well as if he had been in the street listening to them, what they were talking about, and he knew it was not about abandoned farms. He jerked himself around so he could shut the sight from his eyes. He did not wish to see them nor to think of them.

"Leave them be," Thede said, "and finish telling me what you started to say. There might be some sense to your talk after all."

"All right," Ben said, "if you're anxious to know how it could happen that Autumn Hill will be abandoned when the time comes, I'll tell you exactly how. Now, take your girl. Jean, you named her. She's getting married to Frank Gervais, next week, and they'll be moving to the farm they have bought in the east part of the town. And that's where they'll stay. Frank Gervais wouldn't care to have a thing that you are done with. He is going to build his own farm. Someday they'll be putting up a fine house there, maybe even finer than yours at Autumn Hill, and Jean will stick right by Frank. They won't go back to your place to live when you've finished with it. They wouldn't have something that you've finished with, Thede. They won't have anything to do with something that they didn't make themselves. They wish to have a farm and buildings of their own making. That's the way young people like them are.

"And on the other hand, your boy, Howard, is the same

[148]

way. He wants to be a bridge builder, a civil engineer, I've heard. Well, if I'm not mighty much mistaken, he'll be one, unless something unforeseen happens to him. He'll go off somewhere to study, and when he gets through learning how to build bridges, he won't come back to Autumn Hill to build them. He'll go and live where there are bridges needing building. We couldn't help him any here. He'll have to go where he can do his work. So when your boy and girl leave home, you can put it down somewhere that they won't be back again, at least not to stay. They'll be too busy making their own way to come back and live on a farm that hasn't been used in so-many years.

"Now, that ought to convince you that I know what I'm talking about when I say Autumn Hill won't stand so very long after you're dead. And it won't, either. It'll rot to the ground just as quick as all the other fine places here have. You won't be here to see it, Thede, but some of the younger people will, and they'll think of Thede Emerson when they ride past Autumn Hill and stop to look around in the tangle of white birches for the site where the buildings used to stand. It's hard for you to see it, and to believe it, but it's all true. It's just as true as what you yourself might say of the abandoned Hopkins and Edwards places out there next door to you."

Thede had been listening attentively to every word Ben said. There were some things he wished to protest against, but nevertheless he gradually felt himself accepting Ben's prophecy of the future. However, he could not give in completely. He had to say something in defense of the Emersons and of Autumn Hill. After all, he held himself responsible for the house and family name.

"Howard is staying home," Thede said briefly. "And Rosa will be living thirty-forty years from now. She'll live in the house and keep the buildings in repair, even if nobody else does."

"May be making Howard stay home for the time being, Thede, but I'm here to lay you a good-sized bet that he won't be there long, or else I've been mighty much fooled by the boy. I've seen young men like him before, and I'll take a risk on him. He's not the kind to give in like that, after he's had his mind bent on bridge building for all these years. Even when he was no more than ten-eleven years old, he used to come in here and when I'd ask him what he was going to do when he grew up to be a man, he'd say he was going to put up big bridges across rivers like the Kennebec and the Penobscot and the Androscoggin. That's what he used to tell me, and he's just as crazy about doing such things now as he ever was, even a lot more so, from what I've heard him say during the past summer."

"And Rosa —"

"Don't try to fool yourself, Thede Emerson. Rosa will be up and out of that house before the year is over. I've heard you say that yourself. So you know it's so. If you were to die this same evening, she'd be up and out of that fine house before your body was cold. And out of it to stay, too. She wouldn't come back.

"I don't like to say such things right to a man's face, but this time I've got all the proof I need to back me up. If what happens between now and spring doesn't bear me out, then I'll let you, and anybody else who has a mind to, call me a liar, and a poor one at that. Rosa won't be there thirty-forty years from now; she won't be there much longer than three-four months from this time. She'll be living in somebody else's house, maybe pretending to be his housekeeper, but just the same she'll be in another house living as some other man's woman. And I know what I'm talking about. I've lived long enough in this life and in the town of Clearwater to know what's going to take place a long time before it does. Rosa won't be there this time next year, and you can lay bets on that yourself, if you have a mind to. If you didn't have all the money you have, she'd divorce you, but she's got sense enough not to injure her chances of getting a large share of your estate when you die. After you are dead, she'll marry, but not a day before that time.

"Wouldn't be saying all this to you, Thede, if I wasn't positive about what I'm talking. But I am positive, and the proof's not a thousand miles away. I've said all this for your own good, just so you will know how to conduct yourself hereafter. Me and you have been friends all our lives, for the past fifty-sixty years, and I'm tell this to you because I know nobody else will come out and say it to your face. There's any number who will say it behind your back, like all gossip is done, but I can tell it to you face-to-face and back the truth up with proof, if you demand it."

By the time Ben had finished and settled down in his buggy-backed chair to wait for Thede to comment on what he had said, the store was almost empty. One by one the men had gone out, most of them having already heard several times before much of what Ben had said, and when Thede looked around to see who was present, only he and Ben were left. Outside in the street, several men were talking about something else, no longer interested in Thede's affairs.

Ben watched Thede and waited for Thede to try to refute his statements. He waited a long time, and still Thede said nothing. Thede was thinking carefully about all he had heard. Ben had spoken convincingly, so convincingly that he gradually had to confess to himself that there was a lot of truth in what he had been told, much more than he was willing to admit.

He did not believe everything Ben had said, however. The things he did not like to admit, he always rejected as being untrue. Many times, as now, he had been confronted with a statement of fact, backed up with an abundance of irrefutable proof, but if it had not suited him, he had steadfastly refused to acknowledge the truth of it.

While Ben watched his face, Thede tried to keep from showing his thoughts. However, deep within himself he felt sad, and he realized that it was too late now to do anything about his life. He knew he could never overcome what was coming as surely as the next winter's snow. His children hated him, and undoubtedly they had a right and just cause to do so, and Rosa had always been tricky and deceitful, going her own way, getting what she wished at any cost, regardless of what he would have her to do. Since the first time she had been unfaithful, he had known exactly the kind of woman she was, and he had allowed her to do as she pleased in order that she would work for him. He had made Rosa what she was.

No other word passed between Thede and Ben. What

had been said was final as far as Thede was concerned, and Ben held his tongue. Ben was afraid now that perhaps he had gone too far, and that he had made another enemy for life. Although he had no way of knowing otherwise, Thede was grateful to him. He wished then that Ben had had the courage to say such things to him fifteen years earlier. If Ben only had, he knew that he might have conducted his farm and his family relationship altogether differently. He might have won and held the love of his wife and children, instead of living to be hated and cursed by them. But perhaps he was just getting old; in his heart he knew that it would not have been different.

With only a glance at Ben, which Ben at once understood to show Thede's appreciation for what he had said, Thede got up and walked stiffly out of the store and toward his car in the street.

All the way home he could think of nothing else. Every word that Ben had said reminded him of what might have happened differently, and of what would surely take place in the future. He did not know what he could do to stop the inevitable course of events, yet he wished to stop it and to divert it, more than he could remember ever having wished to do anything in his past sixty-odd years. Secretly, deep within himself, he knew it was now too late to do anything about it; what was to happen had been foretold. It was inescapable.

On his way home, driving his old car slowly over the rough town road to Autumn Hill, he tried to decide what to do about the future. He could partly regret the harm he had done but, as it had already been incurred, he knew of no way to rectify it. It was too late to make any kind of apology to his children, the two whom he believed he had actually injured the most. The one act of his life that he could look back upon and call good, and for which he was thankful, was his consent to allow Jean to marry Frank Gervais. He happened to remember, however, that the act had not been prompted by any motives of love for her. He had given her permission to marry Frank solely because he wished to get her off his hands so he could save the expense of keeping her there, and Gervais had been the most likely man who could and would support her.

But Howard — It was even too late to let Howard have the money he needed. It was nearly two weeks too late now. If Ben Robinson had awakened his mind two weeks earlier, he might have done something. As it was now, Howard would remain at home another year, and even if he should go to Autumn Hill at that moment and tell Howard that he could have the money the following year, Howard would suspect, and rightly so in the light of the past, that his father was trying to get him to do the work that winter under a false promise. Howard would never believe him now. Thede could not blame Howard for taking that attitude; he had deceived Howard too many times in the past in order to get more work out of him.

Long before he reached Autumn Hill, driving slowly through the new forest on the narrow road, Thede began to feel for the first time what it was like to be alone in the world and to know that while he lived he would never be able to have the love and companionship of his family. He was hated; he knew now that he deserved to be hated. No one respected him, and he might have had the love of his wife and children as long as he lived. It was too late. He would have to endure perhaps another ten years of the same life he was accustomed to. He was old now, deserted by his wife and children, and helpless to do anything about it.

CHAPTER XV

AT LAST, AFTER MONTHS OF WAITING THAT SEEMED TO JEAN like years, the wedding day had arrived. She knew that it was a morning in October and that the trees were turning and that it was cooler than it had been before that fall. She knew then that, although it was apparently like most October days, this one was like none other she had ever known.

Outside the leaves were falling; orange, red, brown, and yellow leaves twisted and twirled in the air. When it looked as though every tree had shed all it possibly could, more leaves came down in clouds of red and yellow, blowing across the dooryard and against the sides of the house, and embedding themselves around the building as though they were trying to add to the warmth within it. Thede and Howard had already banked the house for the winter and now the leaves were covering the unsightly sawdust until none of it could be seen.

Everything was ready for the marriage ceremony that evening at seven. Everything that could be thought of had been done, many touches given several times over, and Jean finally agreed that the plans and decorations were as perfect as she could make them. Rosa had been busy, too. She had been baking since the early forenoon of the day before, and cakes, pies, meats, sauces, all were ready or would be by midafternoon. For once Rosa had actually tried to make the house as pleasant and as comfortable as she knew how. All that week she had been working from dawn to late in the evening arranging furniture and decorations.

In all the rooms downstairs Jean and Howard had placed branches of autumn leaves. There were such clusters of them all over the walls and on the tables that the entire house seemed to be in the heart of a young maple grove. Even the kitchen was full of color, and the hall was lined with leaves from floor to ceiling. It had always been the custom in Clearwater to decorate the interiors of houses with maple leaves for a fall wedding and Rosa had been determined to see to it that her house was as profusely and as tastefully decorated as any had ever been in town. She was proud of Autumn Hill, now that so many guests would be there for several hours, and she wished the people to know that she could plan and carry out a wedding, with a supper and celebration, as well as, if not better than, any other housewife present.

Howard had raked the leaves again the day before, carrying them to the road to be burned as fast as they fell. When he removed the old leaves, the ones that had been lying on the lawn from two days to a week, the new ones that fell incessantly from the trees covered the grass with splotches of red and yellow. He had mown the grass again that day, too, and now, after twenty-four hours, the lawn was smooth and green. The falling leaves sprinkled it during the forenoon and afternoon until it looked like a colorful comforter in a warm bedroom.

There was no doubt of the size of the crowd that would attend the wedding. Thede had seen to that. He had been inviting people for more than three months, telling them that for once in their lives they would be given the opportunity of taking part in a wedding celebration that they would long remember and talk about. His last-crop cider has appealed to the men and boys, and the unusual sight of seeing an Emerson girl marry a Frenchman was enough to excite the curiosity of all the women and girls and bring them to Autumn Hill from most of the villages and towns within easy traveling distance. Thede said that he was certain that no less than five hundred people would be there, and that he had enough cider for six hundred if the women would content themselves with one or two glasses, and if the men did not drink more than three or four. But there was to be no limit to the quantity of cider a man might drink. Everyone could drink until he had all he wished, even if Thede had to give away the last drop his cellar held. He knew he would be able to get more, because the new-crop cider was already on its way, and he would fill up his empty barrels with the new when the old was gone.

Jean was far too busy with her preparations to think about the house or the decorations or the food any more. She had left everything in her mother's care, and she was free to stay upstairs in her room where she could lay out her wedding garments and watch them until the time came for her to begin dressing. There would be many women and girls there early in the afternoon who would be glad to help Rosa downstairs.

The weather could not have been more favorable. A cool north wind swept over the Hill, shaking trees free of leaves and making the warmth from the stoves pleasant for the first time that fall. A light frost earlier in the week had foretold a cool wind for the coming days. Whenever there was a north wind in October, everyone knew that there would be pleasant weather for several weeks. The air would be cool and dry, and the nights would be clear and frosty. After the first of October, the wet mists of summer vanished with the new season, and the field grass remained dry. One could walk across the fields now without coming home with wet feet.

Jean had taken an early-morning walk before breakfast, running across the frosty grass and down over the hillside and back again until she felt gayer than she had ever felt. But, she told herself, never before had she been nearly married to Frank. She did not know at first that what had made her feel so young and so glad was that she and Frank would soon be alone together in their own home.

After she had returned to the house, her face flushed from running up the hillside, she fell across her bed and closed her eyes. She wished to find herself alone with Frank. After that she did not know how she could wait until late that evening; it seemed such a long way off then.

For the first time since anyone could remember, fires had been made in every stove in the house. It had never happened before, in Jean's and Howard's lifetime. There were six stoves, including the range in the kitchen, and Thede devoted most of the forenoon running back and forth to see that the draft on each stove was set in precisely the right position and that the fireboxes held sufficient embers and fuel. In between times he carried in large armfuls of seasoned chunks of maple, white birch, and beech. These were piled in neat stacks behind the stoves, ready and at hand when more fuel would be needed. He was more concerned about having the house thoroughly and comfortably heated than about anything else then. It did not matter that the doors were left open; the outside doors had to be open, he said, until the house every room and corner of it, was warm and dry. The people of Clearwater would appreciate Autumn Hill all the more when they had gathered in a warm dry house. He was determined that each man, woman, and child should go away later that evening saying how much he liked the Emerson home.

Row after row of cups, glasses, and mugs lined the cellar walls. They had been carefully washed, wiped, and polished several days before; and clean sheets of newspaper had been spread over the shelves and over the upturned bottoms. Every cider barrel in the cellar had been tapped. Thede had first tasted a quarter-glass from each barrel, and then had inserted a wooden spigot so that there would be no delay when his friends and guests came down to drink his good cider. Two small, copper-bound oak kegs had been filled with apple juice and carried upstairs to the dining room. This was the cider for the women and girls. Rosa had set several trays of glasses beside them and Jean had arranged the table with a lace cover.

The food that Rosa had prepared for the supper, which was to follow immediately after the wedding ceremony, was put away in the pantry, ready to be carried out and served. Rosa had baked pies and cakes for two whole days. Pumpkin, cranberry, mincemeat, chocolate, apple, lemon, berry, and raisin pies were stacked three and four layers deep on the pantry shelves. And there beside them, wrapped in cloths, were thick fragrant cakes; there were coconut, pound, chocolate, angel's food, and cream cakes, still as fresh as they were the moment they were removed from the oven.

Pans of roast chicken, turkey, and duck were covering an entire table in the pantry, and on another table there were large covered dishes containing baked ham, beef, and lamb. In the kitchen, ready to cook later in the day, were pans of shell beans, potatoes, cabbage, squash, and corn. There were many other prepared dishes, too; everywhere in the kitchen and pantry was food that was waiting to be cooked at the proper time.

But above all, in the baking range, were eight large earthen pots of beans, and as many more pans of brown bread. No matter what else Rosa had to serve, and no matter how abundant it was, she had put the greater part of her time on baked beans and brown bread. She would have felt that she had disgraced herself if that had been missing from the tables. People who liked baked beans and brown bread accepted no substitute, even at a wedding supper. And a wedding supper, like any other meal at the end of the week, would not be complete without them. The baked beans and brown bread had been prepared with greater care and attention than had any delicate cake or complicated sauce.

There would be room for everybody inside the house, and even though barely more than two hundred could crowd into the dining room and hall and kitchen for the supper, there would be seats where everyone could sit with his plate and his mug of cider or cup of coffee and eat in comfort. On the rear porch Thede had built three rows of benches. There were even more spaces provided in the yard, where Howard had arranged boxes and boards to seat all who could not find chairs in the rooms and on the porch.

Nothing, it seemed, had been overlooked now. With a week's preparations, Thede said that no man ought to overlook anything, not even the minister to marry the boy and girl. The minister would be there, because he had been engaged long before October, and Thede knew there was no danger of his failing to get Jean married to Frank Gervais before the evening was over.

Once that very thing had occurred in Clearwater and Thede was not the kind of man to forget it. All the guests had assembled at John Childs's to witness the marriage of Jake Cram and Susan, John's oldest daughter. Everything had been provided for, so the Childses thought, but when the time came to perform the ceremony, there was no minister present. In the haste and excitement of getting Susan married to Jake Cram, the minister had been forgotten. They did not postpone the celebration, however, and everything else was carried out according to the plans, even Jake and Susan's overnight honeymoon at a tourist camp on the Lewiston highway. A week later John got the minister, who performed the delayed ceremony. But Thede had no intention of having anything such as that mar his plans. There would be no cause to postpone the wedding so long as he had charge of it. The minister would be there if he was alive at the time. Thede would see to that.

Howard had been working that week much harder than he had labored during the past summer for the town on the roads. He had been up at five every morning doing everything that Jean, Rosa, Thede, or he himself could think needed to be done. Each forenoon and afternoon he had constructed benches, cleaned rooms, built shelves in the kitchen and pantry to hold the quantities of food, moved chairs and tables from room to room, carried out pieces of furniture that would not be needed and which otherwise would have stood in the way.

Even after all that had been finished, when they thought of more things to be done, Howard did them. He did not object to the work, because he liked to do it for Jean; Jean felt so sorry for him at times, seeing him laboring day after day for her, that she could not keep from crying when she remembered what must have been on his mind all that time. Not once, however, did she say anything to him about it, because she knew it would hurt him more and make matters worse for him than they already were. Neither did Howard mention the thoughts in his mind; but Jean knew all the time that he wished to be in Boston going to school. After that night when they had the argument with Thede, it seemed as though there was no use in ever again mentioning it. Thede did not bring up the subject, and Howard's mouth was grimly closed.

All during that last day, Jean often stopped in the midst of what she was doing and wondered how she was going to be able to leave Howard there in the house with Thede and Rosa through the coming winter. She did not like to think of it; but even though she closed her eyes tightly, trying to blot out the inevitable picture in her mind, she could not keep from thinking about it. During the past months when she had been planning her wedding, she had not considered Howard as a part of it, because both of them had believed then that he would be away at college. Now she did not know what to think. Howard would not only be present at her wedding, but he would also have to stay there when she and Frank went off to live in their own home.

There would be a time, Jean was positive, when there would be a solution. Eventually Howard would leave. But in the meantime she did not know what would happen to him. They had been together all their lives, living there with Thede and Rosa; and the winters had been lonely even then. She knew that being with Thede and Rosa would be worse for Howard than living by himself in a house. They rarely spoke to Howard, so there was not even conversation for him. Howard could read magazines and books, of course, up in his own room. She could not bear to think how lonely he would be there in the cold house. If there were only something she could do, some way in which she could reveal to him her sympathy and love to help him overcome his loneliness, she wished to do it. If she could have brought him to her room and let him know how she felt toward him, she would have called him at once; but she was afraid to have him there now, she was afraid to trust herself alone with him, for he would have needed all of her sympathy and love.

She caught a glimpse of Howard through the window, but he was lost from sight a moment later in the red foliage of the trees. She knew he was down there in the back yard working for her, trying to have everything in readiness for the evening. Again she wished to call him to her room, this time so much that she even ran to the window and tried to see him. Then she thought of going down into the yard to keep him company while he set the benches between the maples, but she knew that would not be wise, either. The mere fact that she went where he was and stayed with him would make him wonder why she did it. When the excitement of the wedding and the celebration had worn away, he would be more miserable than ever after she had gone if he did find out her motive.

After the forenoon had passed, the day went swiftly. By midafternoon, Jean had tried on her wedding dress several times, taking it off quickly on each occasion when she realized that it was still too early for her to get ready. The last time she had taken the dress off and laid it carefully on the bed beside her white silk stockings, her white kid slippers, her white lace veil, and her white silk underclothing.

There was no space on the bed for her and no other place in the room where she could lie down to rest. She went back to her chair, glancing every few minutes at the clock on her dresser, and then looking out the window where the air was full of maple leaves twirling against the windowpanes and to the lawn below.

Once she was so delighted by the red glow the leaves cast over the walls of the room that she ran to the window, raised it, and leaned far out to catch in her hands as many of the leaves as she could. At the window she saw Howard again; he was hammering nails into the benches between the maple boles. She wished to call him, to tell him to stop what he was doing and come up to her room. When she became fully conscious of what she had been on the verge of doing, she began to tremble so violently that it frightened her. Before Howard could see her, she closed the window and ran across the room with the red and yellow leaves in her arms. She stood beside the bed and dropped the leaves slowly one by one over her glistening white wedding garments. She did not know why she did that, unless she wished them to fall there and lie on the white silk. She thought that the color of the leaves made the whiteness of the silk and softness of its texture seem more beautiful than ever.

After a while she bent over the garments and gathered each leaf separately and carried them all to the dresser where she placed them in her jewel box. She did not know why she was keeping the leaves, or why she would take them away with her, but she knew she wished to have them above everything else in the room. After she and Frank had gone to their new home, she would take them out of the case and spread them on her bed, and the sight of them would make her weep. She did not stop to wonder why they would bring tears to her eyes, but she did know that she would look at the tender leaves in her hands and cry over them. It was something about Autumn Hill, perhaps; possibly something that would remind her of Howard. But whatever the charm it was that the leaves held, she knew she would keep them forever. She would recall Autumn Hill; she would remember the house and more especially her room, her parents, the beauty of the hilltop when the frost was on the grass; the leaves would remind her of Howard.

She could not understand just then what the leaves would mean to her later, any more than she could understand the sudden impulse that had caused her to run to the window and, leaning far out, bring them to her bed to sprinkle over her white bridal clothes. After ten years, perhaps, when both she and Frank had grown older, and when there were children of theirs beside her, she would take the remnants of the leaves from the case and look at them and, she hoped, understand at last what meaning they had held for her all those years.

Jumping up, Jean ran to the window and raised it desperately. She leaned far out trying to see through the mass of maple leaves. Howard was not within sight, nor could she hear the sound of his hammer. She waited as long as she could, her heart beating madly, and then she called him.

"Howard! Howard! Howard!"

She waited breathlessly, her hands clutching the sides of the window, but he did not answer her. She waited for him to answer her as long as she could remain standing on her feet, and when she closed the window, she sank to the floor.

CHAPTER XVI

~~~~~~

Howard, his hands clenched tightly in his pockets, was leaning against a maple tree and staring across the lawn at the brightly lighted house. The crowd was everywhere. Inside the dwelling, men and women pushed and weaved, trying to go from one room to another; and because the porch was filled, groups of men stood at the windows on all sides of the house and tried to see what was happening inside.

Everybody was there that evening to witness the wedding of Jean Emerson and Frank Gervais. Moreover, it was the first time that Erik Hedenstjerna and Axel Nordenskjold had been invited to Autumn Hill. It was the first time that they or members of their families had ever been asked to enter the Emerson home.

Alarak Henata was there with his wife and all his daughters, and so were Henrik Hilditch and Fridtjof Hilditch; the Larsens had come, and also the Hammarstands and Vyssotskys. And others continued to arrive by automobile, by wagon, and afoot. Louis Bedard had been one of the first to get to Autumn Hill, bringing his wife and eleven children. The St. Denis family was there, too, having come in three automobiles. And mingling with the other guests somewhere in the house or around it was the Dube family, the Cotnoirs and Fortiners. But they were not the only guests present. All the Waltons and Frosts and Cliffords were there. Besides these, there were scores of other townsmen, some of whom Thede himself had not seen in ten or fifteen years.

People had come from the surrounding towns, too, as well as from Clearwater and the village. There were times, such as election days, town meetings, Grange fairs, and homecomings, when several hundred people got together for a day; but none of those gatherings could compare with the numbers and the different nationalities milling about Autumn Hill.

Since five o'clock that afternoon more automobiles had used the road to Autumn Hill than had passed over it during the last twenty years. The democrat wagons and buggies were as numerous as the cars. By midafternoon people had started from all directions, coming toward Autumn Hill to attend the wedding and to take part in the celebration that was to follow the supper. But the marriage of Jean and Frank was not the only reason why so many men and women were there; the townsmen wished to be present to see the foreigners enter Autumn Hill and to witness an Emerson marry a Frenchman. The townsmen had to come; it was the one event that year they could not miss seeing.

Howard sat alone, watching it all from his seat at the maple tree.

Half an hour later somebody came out of the darkness behind him and almost stumbled over his feet.

The other man shaded his eyes and peered at Howard until he recognized him.

"What's the matter there, Howard? Have you been drinking too much of the old man's cider?"

Howard laughed good-naturedly. John Childs motioned toward the road behind him.

"I've got a few bottles of beer down there under the bridge. Care for some?"

"I guess not," Howard said. "I don't care for anything to drink just now. There ought to be one sober man around here tonight."

John dropped down on the ground beside Howard, glancing around to see if there was anyone near them.

"Just saw Leland down the road near the stream," he whispered. "There was somebody with him."

"You don't have to tell me who it was. I know."

"Do they go out together like that all the time?" John asked. "Heard a lot about Rosa and Leland in the village, sitting in Ben Robinson's store and listening to the talk, but I never paid much heed to the gossip. Thought it was just a lot of talk about nothing half-truthful."

"We don't have to talk about that," Howard said. "It's bad enough having a mother who behaves like a bitch. Let's let it go this time, John. I don't like to talk about it. You know as much as I do, anyway."

John laughed, but he could not make Howard say anything else as long as that was his attitude.

Presently Howard reached down and pulled up a handful of grass and made a wad of it between the palms of his hands. He rolled the ball tighter and threw it as far as he could into the shadows.

"Are they going to pull that rotten stunt on Jean this evening?" he asked nervously.

"You bet your life they are," John said. "They've got everything all ready for it now. It wouldn't appear to be a consummated wedding if the boys didn't give them a charivari."

"I guess that's what everybody is waiting for now. The supper is over and it's time for them to go away. I wish they would all go home and not do it this time."

"Why?" John asked. "What's wrong with doing that? It's only neighbors and townspeople. And besides, there hasn't been a wedding in the town in the past ten years that the boys haven't had their fun with. It wouldn't be a complete marriage without the stunt, now would it, Howard?"

"Yes, it would, too. The Scandinavians don't do that. Neither do the French and the Russians. And besides, that hasn't anything to do with a marriage. It's just a low-down trick, that's what it is. It's a rotten way to treat people when they get married."

"You're just mad about it because it's your sister who's got married," John said. "You've helped pull the stunt at other weddings, haven't you?"

"I have not."

"Bet you have, too. Everybody likes to see it done. It's the best part of weddings, that and the hard cider, and a little homemade beer to mix with it."

Howard did not have any kind of answer to make. A group of men were coming around the corner of the house just then and they gave him the opportunity to ignore John's reply. The men walked toward Howard and John

Childs and stopped midway between them and the house.

Howard could overhear every word they were saying. They had been talking about the breeding of sheep, but by the time they had lit their cigarettes and pipes, one of them began to say something about Jean and Frank. All of them had been down in the cellar several times already.

"Frank Gervais has a lot coming to him," one of the men said, "and he ought to be proud of it. He doesn't know yet how lucky he is to get Thede Emerson's consent to marry Jean and take her away to himself. Thede is the last man in Clearwater I'd ever thought would let a Frenchman marry his daughter."

"Used to think about upsetting her myself," another man said. "Guess I'd have tried if I had thought there was a chance. Never was able to figure out whether Thede wished to marry her off, or whether he would rather keep her for himself."

"The young girl never gave you leave to upset her, did she?"

"Well, not precisely."

"If I were you then, I should stick to the woman you've got. It's going to be a cold winter that's coming on, and you don't wish to live by yourself, do you? No! I didn't think you did. You can leave your wife, but that's as far as you'll ever get with the Emerson girl. She's going to stay married to Frank Gervais. I'm here to tell you that. French and Scandinavian men know how to keep their women. They treat them so good they don't have a mind to leave. I'm talking about the French and Swedes and Danes and the Norwegians. Can't say that about the Finns and Russians. Can't understand those creatures. Sometimes I get to thinking that maybe the Finns and Russians aren't human. They sure don't act like humans sometimes. You get a Russian or a Finn mad about something in the woods, and let him get his hands on an ax, and God Himself wouldn't be responsible for his actions. The French and Swedes, yes. But the Finns and Russians I can't say about."

Fred Cram had evidently been drinking several bottles of beer in addition to Thede's cider. He reeled around several times, finally clutching at the arms of his friends.

"Gather close around me," he said. "Got something to say to all of you here this evening."

"You're not telling any secrets, are you, Fred?" somebody asked him. "They're hard things to come by and I wouldn't turn them loose if I didn't know what I might say."

"May, in the State of Maine," Fred began, "is the time of year when the men and women on the farms and hills in the back-country thaw out and begin to live again. Some of them get winter-killed, just like the lawn grass does if the ground gets wet and freezes before snow flies, and they never are able to get up and out till the month of June. But May is the time of the year when most townsmen thaw out. The warmth of the new summer creeps into their blood, and sometimes into their heads. The ground thaws in April, but it's not till May that the townsmen walk out-of-doors bareheaded and begin to remember that it's time to buy a new supply of auto grease. After May comes a long row of months made for good living. That's the time when the townsmen make

[173]

up their minds about doing something. In May comes the time for love-making, ground-breaking, seeding, and auto-greasing. Auto-greasing starts in May and it keeps on after that head start until by midsummer the greasing and oiling that's done takes up everybody's time and there's no time left to do anything else."

Everybody laughed and several men slapped Fred on his back.

"That's a pretty speech, Fred. Can't you tell us some more? You're not done yet, and so soon, are you?"

"Take care," Fred said. "Got more to tell you. May is the time to grease the autos and make them run fast, but all that greasing leads up to the month of October. It's in October when the townsmen get a little weary of auto-greasing, and then they decide to settle down and rest a little. Well, a man can't get a complete and satisfying rest without a woman to make him comfortable, so that's why townsmen get married here in the back-country in October. Bet nobody ever thought of that before. But it's the real and true reason why people get married in October. They see that winter's coming and they take care. They're tired of greasing autos for riding, so they just get married to shut down the summer. Thought I'd tell you people why so many townsmen get married in October. Didn't wish any enemies to be made by my talk. Just would like everybody to know what makes the townsmen get married. It's to keep us warm in winter, so we won't get winter-killed like the lawn grass does in my yard. And besides that, it gives us a good rest after so much auto-greasing all summer. You can store the auto and go into your house and stay till spring, and your wife won't let you get winter-killed in spots."

"That was a real pretty speech, Fred," someone said, "and it sounded nice to listen at, but it doesn't make much sense to an old man like me. Haven't got an auto to grease, and I was winter-killed in spots eleven-twelve-thirteen years ago. You must be drunk to talk like that, so I guess that we should go down into Thede's cellar again and have another round so we can listen to you with more appreciation. Couldn't make any sense out of a word you said. Now, when you were speaking of the Finns and Russians just a while ago, I knew durn well what you were talking about. You take a Finn or a Russian and turn him loose where trees are growing, make him mad about something or other, and then give him leave to put his hands on an ax — Good God! Chances are, there won't be any trees left standing, or you, either. If you've got a fondness for living any longer, you'll run for your life like you've never run before."

"That's right," Fred said. "Let's run for our lives to the cellar. But we've got to make haste, because we don't want to miss seeing the stunt take shape in the house. It ought to be ready to come any minute now."

CHAPTER XVII

~~~~~~

HOWARD WALKED TO THE FRONT DOORSTEP AND LOOKED down the hall. He saw that preparations for the charivari were being made upstairs, and that all that now remained was for Jean and Frank to start to their room. Upstairs on the second floor a crowd of young men and girls, all of whom Howard knew, were laughing and running from room to room. The people downstairs waited eagerly for something to happen.

The guest room on the right of the landing was the one that Jean and Frank would occupy for the night. Rosa had decided that they must remain at Autumn Hill that evening instead of going to the other part of town where their new home was. Rosa had said that if they did not stay there for the night, people who had come to the wedding expecting to see Jean and Frank initiated by their friends would be disappointed. Rosa hoped all the guests would have a good time in her house, so they would go away talking about her. She had insisted on their remaining until the following day over the objections of both Jean and Frank. They had at last given in to her, but far from willingly, and had promised to stay for the night.

There was no way of knowing then when the charivari would be started. No one seemed to know, but Perley Phillips appeared to have taken charge of everything on the upstairs floor, and he was giving directions to everybody.

Jean and Frank were still in the dining room, where the supper dishes had been removed for the reception, and they did not appear to be anxious to leave. The people who were waiting had to stand in the hall until they came out of the dining room and started up the stairway. That was the moment when the fun would start.

Howard stood alone, backed against the door, silent and gloomy. He tried not to let anyone stop and talk, because he did not feel like listening to what anybody had to say to him.

Others around him, jammed tightly, were far from being silent. Most of them were talking as loud as they could in order to make themselves understood above the uproar in the hall. Everyone was trying to talk at once, and no one seemed to know or to care what the other person was attempting to say. The prospect of seeing the charivari begin at any moment was enough to distract whatever attention there was.

Behind Howard was a group of men who had been talking ever since he came into the hall. He turned around to see who they were, since it was impossible to escape overhearing what they said. Ben Robinson was among them, and Arthur and Lincoln. Alarak Henata was standing on the edge of the group with Axel Nordenskjold.

"Well," Ben was saying, "there's going to be one house in town that won't be dark this winter. I tell you,

Arthur, it looks like to me that every year brings ten-eleven more dark houses, and the end isn't in sight yet, not by a long sight. The townsmen all die off, or move to Portland to spend the winter in hotels where I'm told they have steam heat and running hot water all night long, and that makes more dark houses than ever during the winter. Of course, it's a little different in summer, because summer-people from Boston and New York and Philadelphia who have bought farmhouses and built camps on the lakes make a lot of lighted buildings then. But, somehow, that isn't the real thing. They are just summer-people, staying here for a month or two, maybe three-four. The townsmen are the ones I'm concerned about. If it wasn't for young people like Thede's daughter and Frank Gervais marrying and making homes of their own, the whole place would be empty of true townsmen in another twelve-thirteen years. The taxes are piling up hand over hand every year, with nobody left living to pay them. This was once a fair-sized town, and the village was a hustling little place in those days, but it's all gone now. The rats will be carrying off the rest of us some day, if we don't take care."

"It's men like Alarak and Axel, there, who are the only people left to save the town," Lincoln said. "If it wasn't for the Henatas and Nordenskjolds living here, we might just as well stop trying to run a town any longer. It's people like them who are paying seventy per cent of the taxes now, and every year that passes makes it a little bit more. Just look around you here and see all the Hammarstands and Hedenstjernas, Nissens, and Cotnoirs present at this wedding party! There's more of them here this evening than there are of us. That's a fine sight for us to see, but there's no way of bettering it."

He stopped and looked over the heads of the crowd, trying to see if Thede were in the hall at that moment.

"We ought to be glad to see them," Lincoln continued, "though I guess Thede has sort of seen black spots before his eyes every time he has heard Hormidas Doucette say *'Comment ça va'* in his house this evening. Who would ever thought the time would come when French and Swede and what not would be heard in the Emerson house! Never thought I should live to hear foreign languages spoken at Autumn Hill."

Alarak Henata caught Ben Robinson's eyes.

"I'm going to get those sheep next week," he said. "Me and my oldest son are making the trip out to Montana to buy forty head of ewes and a ram. They'll cost me a great deal of money, but I'm going to have the best sheep I can put my hands on."

Ben glanced uncomfortably at Arthur, and then at Lincoln Burton. He did not know what to say.

"You shouldn't own such fine sheep, Alarak," Lincoln said. "You'll make Thede Emerson think that you're a better stockman than he ever was."

"I'm not trying to make as much money as he did," Alarak said seriously. "But I like fine sheep. I'm going to have fine sheep."

There was complete silence in the group for several minutes. Finally Arthur White got ready to continue the conversation that had been interrupted by Alarak Henata's talk of sheep.

"Got no objection to anybody paying taxes," he said,

"but that doesn't give them leave to run the town, too. It's getting so that a townsman in Clearwater might just as well go bellow down a well for all the good thinking about securing a political office will do him. There's two French selectmen right now running the town and it looks to me like there's going to be another one after spring election. You take the town's paying jobs, which we pay taxes to provide, and look at who's holding them now. There's the road work, and a Swede is running all the road work for the town and getting paid nine dollars of our money a day for it. That's what it has come to. Guess we're just about done for. I've tried and tried, for I don't know how long, to get a gravel-hauling contract for the roads, and I haven't got so much as an offer. Why? Because the Swedes and Finns and Russians have got all the work for themselves. If it was left up to me, I should turn the whole state loose to them, or them loose on the state. It's either going to be the French or the Scandinavians, and of the two I don't much care which one it is that rules. One is about as bad as the other, to my way of thinking, and it's a shame, any way you look at it. Here we are, landowners and taxpayers, or former landowners if we have sold out to the foreigners, and we have just been squashed against the wall. There's not enough of us left now in Clearwater at the present time to vote a true townsman into office, much less get hold of some of the town's paying jobs."

"You're too shortsighted about this thing, Arthur," Lincoln said. "Let the French and Scandinavians run the town, if they have a mind to. It'll save us the trouble of doing it ourselves. Then when we get too old to work, we can all go live on the town and have the foreigners support us in comfort. That's the way I'm in favor of doing. Let them run the town all they wish to, but make them support us when we get too old to work and make a living."

"It's either the foreigners or the rats," Arthur said. "One or the other, it's bound to be in the end. The rats have overrun the town just as bad as the foreigners have, and I guess if it comes right down to a choice of one or the other, most of us will choose the French and Scandinavians, because the rats don't and won't pay taxes. Then when the time comes when we can't work any longer, like Lincoln was saying, the rats couldn't support us, but the French and others would be compelled to. The state would make them take care of us, even if they didn't have a mind to. But all the same it's not right. Americans ought to run the town and state. This part of the State of Maine is getting to be more like a foreign country every day. Pretty soon won't any more English be spoken. Nobody will be able to recall our language and say the words we are familiar with. We shall all have to learn French, or some kind of Finnish jabber, and even then we won't be better off, because they tell me that there are Swede-talking Finns and Finn-talking Finns and the one never knows whether the other is praising or damning him. Never thought I'd live to see the day when I'd have to jabber Canuck talk, or something else just as bad, but I see now that it's in sight already."

"The French are all right," Ben said. "There's nothing wrong with them, or any of the others, either. If it wasn't for men like Alarak Henata and Axel Nordenskjold, I'd have to sell out my stock of goods and close up my store."

"As taxpayers, yes. But as neighbors and townsmen, no. Do you know, Ben Robinson, that half of the old families in Clearwater have already got French blood in them? Just take Thede's daughter, Jean. She's married Frank Gervais this evening, and before the coming year is over there'll be a young one half-and-half. That's the way it is getting to be all over these days. If it keeps up, there won't be anybody left with pure American blood in their bodies. Everyone will be half this, that, or the other thing, until finally they'll all be foreign of some kind."

"That's right," Ben said, "and with a little rat on both sides of the family."

"You say that for a joke, Ben," Arthur said, "but it's not going to be funny at all. The rats are worse every year. They come down to my place now and scratch on the door like hungry dogs to be allowed inside. God only knows what they'll be up to next. Maybe they'll set out poison for all of us and take complete possession. We've got to take care."

Alarak Henata moved away to join another group of men on the other side of the hall. He wished to talk with someone who was interested in sheep raising.

Howard had been listening to every word that was said. Every time a group of townsmen got together they joked about rats and cursed foreigners. It was inescapable. No one seemed to be interested in anything else; and their concern for what would eventually become of the town, its complexion and nature, was of momentous importance to all. Howard liked to listen to their arguments, because he had learned many things about people he had never been able to discover by other means. It was at such times when men were completely off their guard, and they told more about themselves than they did about the subject they were discussing.

He hoped they would continue talking, but just then Perley Phillips started down the stairs and a hush fell over the hall. Everyone pushed forward to see and hear what was about to happen.

"The room upstairs is all fixed, folks," Perley said. "And it's getting late. Guess it's about time for people like Jean and Frank to go get in bed."

CHAPTER XVIII

WHILE PERLEY WAITED FOR JEAN AND FRANK TO START toward the stairs, he leaned over the railing and whispered down into the hall.

"We put a gallon of sand in the bed," Perley said, "and the covering is all sewn up tight. Just wait till they come up here and try to get in between the sheets!"

The guests laughed again, and then listened for what Perley had to say next. Perley was the one who always took charge of charivaris, and he knew more about planning them than anyone else. He was always thinking up a new detail to add to the store he had accumulated.

Howard leaned back against the door and waited to hear what Perley was going to say. All around him in the hall the townsmen were having the time of their lives; everyone except himself and the Swedes. The Scandinavians could find no humor in a charivari, and he could not laugh at the jokes planned for his sister.

Jean and Frank came to the door and stopped. They looked at the crowd around the stairway, and they hesitated about going farther. Presently someone behind gave them both a shove and pushed them out into the hall.

After they had once started for the stairs, there was no way for them to turn back. People quickly closed in behind them and, except for the narrow lane through the crowd to the stairway, they were hemmed in on all sides.

Two or three of the girls and Perley Phillips laughed out loud and in a few moments the townspeople were yelling and shouting. It was the signal for everybody to have a good laugh at Jean's and Frank's expense.

"Come on up!" Perley yelled down at them. "Don't hold up the fun! Come on up!"

Again someone pushed them from behind, and they found themselves at the bottom steps of the stairs.

"Let's have it down here!" a man standing in front of Howard yelled.

Howard felt himself being pushed and squeezed in the crowd that surged around him. Everyone was trying to get closer to the stairway.

"Here it comes, folks!" Perley shouted. "Take care down there! Here it comes!"

Jean buried her head against Frank, and Frank stood looking at the people around him without a single change of expression coming over his face. He was prepared to go through with the ordeal, no matter how much he wished to get Jean out of it. There was no means of escape; the only way open for them now was up the stairs. But even though he tried to run up with Jean, somebody still held them back.

All eyes were looking up at the stairhead where Perley and the crowd of men and girls were standing. They were holding something behind their backs.

Before either Jean or Frank had expected it to happen,

Perley stooped over and placed a glistening white-glazed chamber pot on the top step and in another moment it was on its way downstairs, bumping from step to step until at last it reached the floor at Jean's and Frank's feet. The chamber had come fast as its momentum had increased, but not a tread was missed on its way down. It bumped loudly on the last step and clattered on the floor in front of them.

A shout went up all over the house, louder than any before then. It was the climax of the wedding and the only entertaining part of the evening. This was what everybody had been waiting for two hours or more to see. And some of the guests had traveled a long way to get to Autumn Hill. This pleased all the guests now, though, and none of them would leave feeling that he had wasted his time in coming so far from home. Frank blushed, and that was the signal for another outburst of shouts and yells. Jean still had her head buried against Frank and she had escaped seeing what had taken place.

"Up the stairs!" Perley called down to them. "Come on up the stairs! Don't be bashful!"

Then Frank did a thing that no person present had ever seen before on such an occasion. Frank reached down, grasped the white-glazed chamber by its handle, and, throwing it over his shoulder, ran up the stairs with Jean.

The townsmen shouted again and applauded with their hands. Others beat against the doors and walls with their fists, kicking the floor with their heels, and whistling shrilly through their fingers. Whether Frank was being cheered for his bravery in picking up the chamber pot and carrying it over his shoulder up the stairs, no one seemed to know at the moment; but his actions at least proved to them that he was no ordinary man. Even Thede felt proud of his new son-in-law when he realized what had happened. Most men, under identical circumstances, had left it lying on the floor, trying to ignore the china pot clammering at their feet. Everyone felt that he had done something to talk about for the rest of the year. It was the first time a thing like that had ever happened in Clearwater.

The charivari at Autumn Hill had been unique. Thede and Rosa beamed with pleasure.

Howard turned and escaped to the cool evening air at the doorstep. He had watched the whole thing in a daze. Now that it was over and done with, he felt a little better. He could not forgive the townspeople in the house for demanding such a thing, though, and he could certainly not forgive Perley Phillips for being the leader of the crowd upstairs; he hated to think that Autumn Hill had become a place where such a trick could be perpetrated and, worst of all, on his sister.

A few minutes afterward, people began coming out of the house, and Howard jumped down from the door-step and ran out into the darkness where no one could see him. He did not know why he did it, but he felt himself crying the moment he left the door.

It was a long time before he could reason out the cause of his crying, and even then he was not certain of it. It was not because of the charivari; at least that was not the only reason. He believed that it was partly because Jean and Frank were now married, and that he would be left alone in the house with only Thede and Rosa there.

After a while he knew that had been the whole cause. All the excitement of the wedding, the preparations leading up to it, and the work he had done for a week preceding it, had made him think of other things; and he had forgotten that Jean was actually leaving. She and Frank would leave the next day and after that he might never see her again. Something might happen that would prevent his ever seeing her again.

The lights of the last homeward-going automobile could be seen down the road over the marsh, but still he did not get up to go into the house. He sat looking down over the hilltop and trying to see far off into the distance.

Far off over the hills toward the east, lights from farmhouses on the ridges blinked and sparkled in the clear frosty air. The night was clear and dark, with only the brightest stars shining down. The evening was dark, but he remembered that on bright nights, when the moon and stars had shone on the lakes below the Hill, the water had looked like patches of broken glass strewn over a smooth lawn reflecting the light from the sky.

He was trying to think of something else, but his mind kept dwelling on Jean. He could think of her then at that moment, upstairs in the room with Frank, and his body stiffened with tension.

Over toward the south, the dim lights of a village could be seen glowing against the low sky. Back behind him, where the forest was deepest, there was neither light nor sound; but Howard knew that in the forest and in the brushy fields and on the hummocky flats, woodchucks were clambering over stone walls and rock ledges, and that foxes leapt high over fallen trees. No one could see such things on a dark night, but he knew that animals were there.

He did not know what time it was when he got up from the lawn, or how long he had sat against the maple tree. When he got up, the house was dark and he had to feel his way through the hall to the stairway.

There was no sound in the room where Jean was. He stopped at the door and listened for a long time. Occasionally he heard the movement of her or Frank's body, the creaking of the bedsprings when one of them moved or turned over, and then he knew that Jean was not asleep.

He did not know what made him stay there; he did not know what had made him touch the panels of the door with his hands. All he knew at that moment was that he must see Jean in order to prove to himself that she was now the wife of Frank Gervais. After that, he would have to force himself to accept the fact that she was married. As it was, though, he still wanted to be with her, to be able to go into her room, to be alone with her. Until he could prove to himself that she was Frank's wife now and that he was not wanted, he knew that he would never be able to go away from the door and leave her alone in the room with Frank Gervais.

He knocked loudly on the door. A few moments afterward the door opened and Jean stood there looking at him.

"What's the matter, Howard?" she asked with a startled expression. He could see instantly that her face was flushed and joyous. "What on earth is wrong?" she said a moment later.

He moved his head slowly from side to side.

"Then why are you here, Howard? You shouldn't be coming here like this."

He could see her plainly then, because she had stepped forward, partly closing the door behind her, and the hall light revealed her plainly. Still silent, he stared at her until she clutched the thin silk of her gown and drew it tightly around her.

"You must go away, Howard," she said to him. "Please try to understand."

He still had not spoken to her, but he had seen what he had come there to see, and he knew it was true. Jean was another man's wife now.

He was turning to go to his own room when he felt Jean's arms around him. She pressed her body upon him and held him close to her while she kissed him. Then suddenly she was gone, and he heard the door close. Howard turned and walked into his dark room and fell headlong upon his bed.

CHAPTER XIX

~~~~~~

THE FIRST SNOW OF THE AUTUMN HAD NOT BEEN EXPECTED
until Thanksgiving or later. There had been previous years
when there were light flurries during the first and second
weeks of November, but generally one could expect
Indian summer to last almost up to the first day of December. In recent years, however, a white Thanksgiving
had come to be expected. Never did any of the early
autumn snows remain on the ground for more than two
or three days, because the earth took a long time to
release its summer heat, and the sun was always warm on
cloudless November days regardless of how frosty the
nights were.

This year there had been predictions for a light snow
in mid-November. Most of the predictions were based
on almanacs; Thede had made a study of the fall and
winter weather predicted in his favorite almanac and he
had stated that he looked for quite a lot of snow before
the first of December.

Howard had been working around the buildings for
several weeks getting the house and barn in readiness
for cold weather. He had finished banking the house

with sawdust and fir boughs, and he devoted most of his time to stacking wood for the range and heaters. The wood had been cut the previous year and sawn stove-length by Dan Smith's traveling wood saw. All summer the sawn wood had been exposed to the sun and wind, and in the early fall it had been split. Now, after filling the woodhouse, Howard carried the rest of it to the shed beside the kitchen where it could be easily reached during the winter.

Thede had spoken of the coming of snow several times during the past weeks, but Howard had not been interested in what he was talking about. He had grown to be disinterested in anything his father said and rarely answered Thede.

"Your sister's married now and gone away from home," Thede said one evening at supper, "and it would be wise for you to give some thought to choosing a wife. We don't want the Emerson family name to be lost, and it's up to you now to keep it alive. I've noticed that the foreigners have the largest families in the town, and for the good of the Emerson name it'll be best if you marry the daughter of one of them. I've cursed the foreigners all my life, and I still don't want to have one of them in my house while I'm alive, but there comes a time for strong blood in any family. I've seen a lot of farmers end up with scrub stock in their pastures just because they didn't have the wisdom to breed their cows and mares to a new bloodline. That's why I want you to go out and find yourself a wife who doesn't have the plague of the name of Walton, or Frost, or the like."

The early snow did come in midmonth, just as Thede

had said it would. A week before Thanksgiving the snow began to fall, blowing out of the northwest in the early forenoon and continuing the rest of the day without pause. On the hilltop, the earth had been cooled by the constant blowing of the north wind, and the flakes remained on the ground without melting immediately. By evening, there were several inches of it on the ground and the skies were leaden. Thede said that lead-colored skies so late in the afternoon meant that the storm would continue through the night, and possibly for another twenty-four hours. Down in the lowlands, along the shores of the lakes and in the marshes, the snow melted almost as fast as it fell. By nightfall, only traces of it were visible down there.

Howard went to bed earlier than usual that evening. He had sat for a while after supper in the room with Thede and Rosa, listening to the rustle of his father's newspaper and to the painful squeaking of Rosa's chair. As much as he already hated Rosa, his hatred increased when he listened to the chair and looked at her. She would not sit in a chair unless it squeaked, and if, for any reason, her favorite rocker lost its squeak, Rosa jerked and twisted, tapped and worked over it until the old squeak had returned or until a new one had developed. Thede was the same way about his newspaper; he invariably rustled the sheets while he was reading, making noise to show that he was occupied. Two or three times that evening Thede had said something to Howard, but only when he demanded an answer did Howard reply. Thede thought he knew what the matter was with him, but he ignored it completely, so certain was he that in the course of the winter Howard would overcome his disappointment and become contented at Autumn Hill.

It was only eight-thirty when Howard left the room and went upstairs to bed.

After he had gone, Thede turned to Rosa.

"He'll feel better after he sees the ground covered with snow tomorrow," Thede said. "When he sees the snow on the ground, he'll become calm. Snow always makes a man satisfied with living. I've seen it happen for fifty years. A man comes to like the snow, and when it isn't on the ground you miss it until it does come. I know how it is. I've been seeing it come and go all these years and I never feel calm any more until it comes and covers the ground."

Rosa rocked back and forth in her chair, the squeaking rhythmic and sharp, while Thede waited to hear if she would say anything. Presently she changed her position, crossing her legs, and breathed deeply.

"Howard isn't as much of a fool as you make out he is," she said. "Howard's thinking all this time of some way to get out of staying here to do the chores. I can read it in his face every time I look at him. He's no fool. Just because he doesn't complain and beg about going off any more is no sign he's finished with what he's been trying all this time to get. All this time he's been thinking about something. I can see that whenever I look at him."

"Won't do him any good," Thede said. "Maybe no harm, either. He'll wear it off after a few more weeks. By the first of the new year he'll be well satisfied and contented. The snow will make him calm."

Rosa said no more. It was her only contribution of the evening to conversation. Thede glanced over and saw the look on her face and he recognized the determination he saw there. He knew then that it would be useless to press his point with her, because even though she might pretend to listen, she would not say another word. Thede went back to his paper, satisfied in his own mind that he had settled Howard's discontent for the last time. A year or two would prove to Rosa that he was right.

When Howard awoke at six o'clock the next morning, he saw the snow drifted against the windows the moment he opened his eyes. Jumping out of bed, he saw that the ground was covered with a foot or more, and that even the trees had much of it clinging to the bare limbs. He looked out at the white hilltop for several minutes before he felt the chill in the room, and he hastily put on his clothes.

He walked out on the rear porch with the milk pail in his hand on the way to the barn. The snow was twelve or fourteen inches deep, but it was not crusted. The sun was beginning to come up in a clear sky, and he knew that by evening only traces of it would be left on the marshes. It was too early in the year for the snow to stay on the ground, especially since the earth was not frozen; but there was the snow to remind him of the rest of the winter that was to come, weeks of snowbound winter. In January, the snow would remain on the ground, crusting whenever the temperature dropped below the thirties and remaining there until fresh snow fell on top. By late winter, there would be several feet of snow covering the country, layers of frozen crust at irregular intervals to a depth of three feet or more. He finished milking quickly. There were only two cows to milk and feed now; two cows supplied an abundance of milk, cream, and butter for the house.

When he reached the rear porch, he stopped to brush the snow from his boots. Over his shoulder he caught a glimpse of the country toward the east. Even the ever-greens had been powdered with the soft clinging snow, and, as far as he could see, there was a covering of white over everything, although the lakes and streams still remained blue green. But it would not be so very long until the lakes froze, and then the snow would cover even them.

There was a new stillness everywhere. The snow seemed to absorb every sound he could make and to subdue it until it was unrecognizable. There was no rustling of leaves, no creaking of tree limbs, no sudden crash of dead wood in the forest, and no sound of deer and moose to be heard. The only sign of life anywhere within sight was the slow curl of pale-blue wood smoke coming from the kitchen chimney where he had made a fire half an hour before. He kicked the snow from his shoes and went inside.

After breakfast, Thede stood at the kitchen window looking out over the north country. The sun had been up an hour by that time and the wet snow had begun to sparkle on the bare maple and elm limbs. He stood looking at the scene until Howard went to the closet for his leather coat.

"Where are you going now?" Thede demanded of him. "It's not cold enough for a leather jacket."

Howard put his arms through the sleeves of the coat

and buttoned it. He reached into the closet and took down the shotgun from the rack.

"I saw a big woodchuck out behind the barn when I was going to milk," he said. "I may be able to get him with this. If I can find him now, I'll get him."

"Don't object to shooting woodchuck," Thede said, "but I want that you should get those potatoes and apples sorted today."

Thede turned back to the window again, his mind free once more. When he first saw Howard putting on the leather coat, Thede had been afraid that he was going to the village instead of staying at home to do the work that had been provided for him. The shooting of the woodchuck would take only ten or fifteen minutes, twenty at the most, and then he would come back to the house and could be put to work in the cellar.

Rosa had already begun to wash the breakfast dishes, and Thede left the kitchen and went into the next room to make a fire in the cast-iron heater. The house was not so chilly as it had been before sunrise, but Thede still felt the need of a fire in the living room.

Howard had been gone almost half an hour and Thede had been listening for him at the door most of that time. He was fretful and unable to sit still enough to read while Howard was wasting time out behind the barn and was not down in the cellar sorting apples and potatoes. There were eight or ten barrels of apples down there that Thede wished sorted and put into the bins, and there were as many more barrels of potatoes also waiting to be put away for the winter. Thede waited for Howard to come back and start to work without further delay. If he had known that Howard would waste all that time looking for a woodchuck to shoot, he would not have allowed him to go.

The fire had begun to heat the room and Thede was reaching down to close the draft when he heard the sound of the shotgun being fired out beyond the barn.

"Guess Howard's got the woodchuck," he called through the door to Rosa. "He never has to take but one shot at anything he aims to kill. Wish he had the time to get six-seven more out there while he was about it, but those apples and potatoes are waiting to be put away in storage."

Rosa came to the door and stood looking at Thede.

"How do you know it was woodchuck he killed?" she said. "Maybe he killed something else."

Before Thede could turn and look at her, Rosa had gone back into the kitchen. He followed her.

"What're you talking about, anyway?" he asked.

Rosa continued to wipe the dishes without looking around at Thede. There was an almost imperceptible shrug of her shoulders that Thede thought he recognized.

"Howard said he was going out to shoot woodchuck, didn't he? Well, what else would he be out there taking shots at? There's no deer up on this hilltop now. Deer are down in the marshes where the snow is melting. Deer never go to a hilltop to find grass and moss when there is a foot of snow on it."

"Why don't you go out behind the barn and see what he killed?" she said, still not looking at Thede.

"Howard'll be here in two-three minutes now. There's

no sense in going out there through the snow to meet him."

He was about to turn and walk back to the living room to see how the fire was heating when he stopped and glanced out the rear window toward the barn. Rosa clattered the dishes and rattled the silver. She put everything away in its place and wiped off the table.

"It's been ten-fifteen minutes since he shot the woodchuck," Thede said. "He ought to be coming back by this time. All those apples and potatoes are waiting to be sorted and put away in the bins."

He stopped and looked again through the window, but still he could see nothing of Howard at the barn.

"Guess I'll walk out there and find out what's been keeping him," Thede said. He opened the door and went out. "Maybe he did shoot deer."

All the time he was tramping through the snow toward the barn, following the trail Howard had broken, Thede was becoming more and more angry because Howard had wasted so much time when he should have been at the house sorting apples and potatoes. He even began to think of what he was going to say to Howard for wasting so much time that early in the forenoon. He was determined to keep him at work so that he would not have much time to waste thinking about going off from home.

When Thede reached the corner of the barn and looked toward the stone wall where the woodchucks sat when they were out foraging for food, he stopped. He looked again, taking a step forward, his eyes squinting through the glare. He had not yet become accustomed to the glare of sun on snow after the green summer months.

"Howard!" he said roughly.

He looked again, squinting his eyes in order to see what was causing Howard to ignore him.

"Howard!" he shouted angrily. "Come and get to work in the cellar! Stop wasting time out here!"

At that moment he saw the gun almost buried in the snow, embedded as though it had been dropped there. Howard was sitting against the stone wall, his feet and legs under the snow, and his head lying on his left shoulder and against one of the stones in the wall. He looked then as if he had been tired and had sat down against the stone wall to rest and had dropped off to sleep a moment later.

"Howard!" Thede shouted. "Howard! Damn you!"

Without speaking again, Thede walked closer to the stone wall and stopped only a few feet from it. He could not say anything else, no matter how much he tried to make himself speak again, although he felt compelled to shout at Howard and to curse him. The anger that had risen steadily within him while he had been waiting in the house for Howard to come back and start to work was blinding and choking.

Thede knew then that Howard had shot himself with the gun. There was the length of apple limb sticking out of the snow at his feet, the other end of which was still grasped in his fingers. The blast of the gun had torn a ragged hole in the new leather coat, ruining it for further wear until it could be mended. The charge had entered Howard's body just below the collarbone.

He bent over and picked up the shotgun to examine

it. The exploded shell had been ejected, but Thede could not find it in the snow. The magazine of the automatic shotgun held two more shells.

Holding the end of the barrel against the hole in Howard's chest, Thede pulled the trigger, bracing the stock against his shoulder. He did not wait to take aim through the sights when he fired the shell, but the charge entered his son's body where the first one had. Without firing again, Thede ejected the remaining shell from the gun and stood it upright against the wall. Not waiting longer, he turned and walked around the corner of the barn toward the house.

He went several yards through the snow and turned around and walked back again. He threw the gun in the snow at his son's feet and, without looking another time, went around the barn out of sight.

Rosa was standing in the center of the kitchen when he entered the room. She watched without speaking while he picked up the broom and brushed the snow from his boots at the door.

"He didn't shoot woodchuck, did he?" she said.

"Guess he didn't," Thede answered. "Didn't find any dead woodchuck out there."

"Didn't shoot a deer, either, did he?"

"Couldn't find the signs of one."

Rosa smiled from the corner of her mouth. She still had not moved and her eyes burned through Thede. He carefully swept out the snow he had tracked on the doorsill.

"Guess you'll have to sort your own apples and potatoes now," Rosa said. "Don't guess you'll care to pay a hired man to do the work for you. You'd have to pay him thirty-forty dollars a month and board. It won't cost you anything to do it yourself."

"Don't guess it'll make much difference if they stay like they are now," Thede muttered wearily. "It won't matter much now, anyway."

"Well, you're the one who ought to know what you'd like done with them. Do as you mind to."

Rosa untied her apron and tucked up her hair, pinning it tightly over the back of her head. Thede could see her walking out of the kitchen toward the stairway in the hall, but he made no attempt to stop her. When she had gone halfway up the stairs to the second floor, she stopped and called down to Thede.

"Best drive to the village and charge the undertaker," she said. "No sense delaying till the ground freezes and be required to preserve him in the cemetery vault all winter till the spring thaw. It'll be a saving of money in the end to tend to it now."

CHAPTER XX

ONE BY ONE THE BLINDS WERE CLOSED OVER THE WINDOWS. Finally, only the two kitchen windows were left to allow the short winter daylight to shine into the house. By the time winter had set in, Thede had closed all the rooms except the kitchen. He prepared one or two meals a day there, and in the evening he lay down on the quilt-covered couch by the range and slept a little during the long night, half an hour or an hour at a time. During his hours of wakefulness he would sit by one of the windows and gaze unseeingly out into the darkness of the night. The short winter days began at eight-thirty in the forenoon and by four or four-thirty twilight came. Most of his time during the day was spent sitting at a window and looking out over the bleak north country where the ground and new forest was deep in crusts and drifts of snow.

Rosa had been away for three weeks and Thede did not know when she would come back home again. He knew that someday she would return for the purpose of hauling away the furniture and the remainder of her personal belongings, and that while she was there she would close the kitchen blinds, fasten the windows, and lock the outside doors.

It was a forenoon in early December when Rosa left, saying nothing of her plans when he attempted to question her. Thede had let her go. He did not care to try to make her stay if she had made up her mind to leave him and live in the village. And even if he had tried to keep her at Autumn Hill, he knew of no means by which to hold her there against her wishes. He had let her go.

"Had my fill of closed back-country roads in winter," she had said. "Over to the village, the state roads are plowed and auto travel is open all winter. Out here at Autumn Hill I wouldn't see anybody till spring. I've had my fill of it for twenty years, and now I'm going out."

Thede had said a few words to her, but his protests were feebly uttered. He did not feel like undertaking the task of trying to persuade her to stay with him even one more year. He had offered to take her on a short trip if she would stay, but nothing could deter Rosa from her plans then. He had told her that after the present winter he would take her down to Portland every year to spend the cold months in a steam-heated hotel. But she would not believe him. She thought he was only lying and making a promise he never intended to keep when the time came to go. She had been listening to such things for twenty years and she was determined not to be fooled any more.

"Go on off," he had told her. "Don't need you here, anyway. You'll be getting in my way all the time and I don't care to have anybody around the house to bother me. Go on off! Stay off! Always liked my own company better than other people's, anyway. Go on off! Stay off!"

Rosa was glad to get it over with so easily, but even

if he had not agreed to her going, she would have left just the same. She would have left at the hour she had set in the first place regardless of anything he was capable of doing to stop her.

Since she had been gone, Thede had become more and more pleased every day that he was alone. He had shut up all the rooms except the one he lived in and he did not have to bother about walking from one room to sleep, to another to read, and to a third in which to cook and eat. He was satisfied with the arrangement and he wondered why he had been able to live with his wife and children cluttering up the house as long as he had.

There would be no necessity for his going to the village until spring. There were enough supplies in the house to last him that long and he had everything he needed. He had his tobacco. The cellar held apples, potatoes, carrots, and squash. In the pantry was enough sugar, coffee, salt, and meat to last him for several months. There would be no need of his going to the village store at any time until spring unless he should wish to go.

Many persons, however, spoke of Thede from time to time.

"The end for Thede Emerson was in sight when he sold his dairy and beef herds," Ben Robinson said in the village. "Any man with goat sense might have known that Autumn Hill wouldn't last any longer than it took the Emersons to go off, die off, or otherwise get rid of themselves. Never seen it fail to happen when a man says he's through with the world and let the world be damned. That was what Thede Emerson said. He said he had got what he desired — which was his money — and he didn't care to have anything else to do with the town, the state, or the nation after that. His girl married, his boy killed himself, and his wife will go to live with Leland Stokes for a while, maybe. Thede Emerson is still out there on that back road, but there's not much of the man left now. That's the way he ordered his life, and I, for one, am in favor of leaving him be."

After the first month's talk in the village, no one said anything more about Thede. He was forgotten for the time being, and only when spring came would anyone take the trouble to inquire if Thede had been seen or heard from.

There were other matters of much more importance to discuss during the winter. Alarak Henata was going to erect a three-hundred-foot sheep and cattle barn, and the Dussaults had bought the hundred-and-fifty-acre farm adjoining theirs and were making plans to enclose the new purchase with woven-wire fences. Ben Robinson had already made up his mind to sell his store to Napoleon St. Denis, and Adelard Lavigne had let the contract for a new ten-room house he would build on the site of the old Phillips homestead on the hill above the village. There was no mention of Thede Emerson's name after that.

At Autumn Hill, Thede had a lot of time in which to think over his past life.

He became more and more given to sitting by the kitchen window and looking out over the crusted snow toward the north country. He had nothing new to think of, and there was little of which he had not grown tired of thinking. There were many times during the day when he sat by the window saying a few words to himself. He never fully realized what it was he was talking about, and he mumbled the words so that he could not even hear himself say them. The sounds came from his lips over and over again day after day as he sat looking out over the crusted drifted snow.

Thede had not willingly thought of Rosa since she had left the house. Once or twice he had seen something of hers that recalled her to his mind, but he rarely wondered where she was or what she was doing. She might have been going to dances in the Grange hall, to bean suppers in the Baptist church, and even taking shopping trips to Lewiston and Portland, but he was not sufficiently interested in Rosa to wonder about her more than that. All that was connected with Rosa he wished to be erased from his mind now. She had never been anything more to him than the woman who did the housework and the woman who had borne him two children.

His son and daughter frequently came into his mind. Jean had wished to marry Frank Gervais, and he had given his permission and consent. She had married him and left Autumn Hill. Thede was glad now to think that he had allowed her to marry Frank Gervais. It had made her happy, and he was satisfied. But she had married a Frenchman. That fact made him miserable.

He could not understand then how he had ever allowed himself to listen for one moment to such a proposal. The French were the one people he hated most in the world, and all other foreigners came close behind. People would speak of Thede Emerson as the townsman who had allowed his daughter to marry a Frenchman; consequently he had to shut himself up in his house, close the blinds, and lower the shades at the windows, so that no chance passers-by would be able to look at him. He could never face the town again, when the whole town knew that he had allowed his daughter to marry a Frenchman. Thede covered his face with his hands, pulling down the shades over the windows lower and lower so that no man could look inside and see him. He was ashamed of being seen now. Men would stop and look at him and point their fingers at him. The Emerson name had been disgraced and Autumn Hill would never again be spoken of with awe and respect.

Cooking and preparing his meals was a simple matter for Thede and he did not find it tiresome. He ate very little; an apple or two a day, two or three potatoes baked in their skins on top of the range, and a slice of ham was enough to sustain him. He did not care for any more than that. He could prepare his daily meal in a few minutes and eat it in almost the same length of time. He was not hungry any more.

The woodhouse held enough fuel to last him through that winter and into the following year. He would not be cold for another year at the most, and by that time he expected Rosa to come back. She would have fuel cut, sawn, and split during the summer for another year's use. Rosa would take care of him. Rosa would not let him freeze.

There were other times, however, when he knew that Rosa would never come back to take care of him. He knew as surely as he knew that he was sitting in the kitchen by the window that Rosa would stay away until he was dead. She had said she would when she had left, but at that time he had neither believed her nor cared. She had lived there in the Emerson house with him for twenty years and he did not like to believe that she would leave him at the time when he needed her care more than he ever had.

One day in January while sitting at the window, he recalled, just as clearly and as unmistakably as if he had at that same moment been in Ben Robinson's store, what Ben had once told him. Thede even raised the window shade for a moment to look around the room to see if Ben had come into the house and spoken to him. As soon as he saw that Ben was not present in the room, he sat down again, but the words kept coming back to him just as distinctly as if they were being spoken behind him.

"The time is coming, Thede Emerson, when you'll be sorry for all you've said about the foreigners. You'll be sorry then, too, for the way you've treated your wife and children. The foreigners are our best friends now, and they are just as good as me or you. They haven't got names like Frost and Emerson, and for that reason you say they're not as good as we are. But they're better men than we are, Thede, because they don't keep their children from going off to college. If their children would like to go away from home to study, then their parents save the money for them to go away. They love their children. They don't try to break them to their will. They know that the young people are the ones who will have to do all the work in the world later on, and they help their sons and daughters get the kind of education they need. If you would let Howard go off to college, you'd feel a lot happier about it when you get old. He won't be satisfied to stay here and do chores for you all his life at Autumn Hill. He's got a mind of his own to follow, and you ought to have the sense to let him use his own mind. You won't be any good for work when you're old. Then it will be the young people who will run the town. You're just making way for another foreigner to take his place in the town when you keep Howard from taking up his chosen work."

Thede did not understand much of that now. He could repeat the words under his breath and see Ben Robinson sitting there in his buggy-backed chair in the store, waving his arms when he became excited. But the meaning of the words Ben spoke was too vague for him to understand. He knew that he had made Howard stay at home and he was proud of his achievement. The fact that Howard was dead now did not matter; the important thing was that he had made the boy do what he wished done. He had told his son to stay at home and do the chores, and Howard had done them up to the day he went out behind the barn and shot himself. If he had given Howard five hundred dollars, he would regret it now and never be able to get over the loss of his money. As it was, he had had his own way with Howard, had saved five hundred dollars from being wasted, and had seen to it that the chores were done twice a day.

Thede mumbled something under his breath that he himself could not hear. He could not even remember what it was he was trying to say. But he felt satisfied. He was pleased with himself for having made Howard stay at home.

Outside the window it had begun to snow again. The flakes came down so thickly that it was impossible to see the elm trees that grew across the front of the yard beside the road. The snow came down slowly in large flakes, clinging to the hedges, trees, and house. It was falling on the crust of last week's snow, and the new fall would probably add five or six inches to the two feet already on the ground.

Once he had got up and had gone to the other window to look out toward the barn. Away off toward the south he could see the smooth frozen lake where the snow was falling. The previous snow had drifted before it had time to crust, and the new fall was covering the exposed patches of wind-blown ice. The trees of the forest in all directions were capped with snow and the stone walls and hedges had been buried beneath it. This was the time of year when everything was covered but the highest trees, making the hummocky ground appear to be as smooth as calm water.

He walked back over the kitchen linoleum to the range. The warmth of the fire was like the gentle caress of a warm spring sun. Although it was earlier than usual, Thede lighted the lamp and placed it on the wide window sill where it would proclaim the pride of the Emersons through the night. It was his duty, as long as he could keep himself alive, to light the lamp at nightfall so that Autumn Hill would never be a dark house to anybody who chanced to be passing by.